HAUNT
YOU HAD YOUR CHANCE TO LEAVE

FAIR'S FAIR
BOOK ONE

AJ MERLIN

DEDICATION

This book is for us. All of us who watch a horror movie and feel like it's only a few lines and one less stabbing away from a really hot dark romance.

You know who you are.

1

I'm not even sure I'm in the right place.

Closing the door of the Uber with my hip, I shove my hands in the pocket of my oversized *Texas Chainsaw Massacre* hoodie and look around the almost empty parking lot. *Am* I in the right place? The address isn't quite what Sienna sent me, but the driver hadn't been able to find the exact street number, so...

The sound of the window rolling down catches my attention and I turn to look at the woman in the driver's seat, who's got a look of worry written clearly on her face. "Are you sure you want me to drop you off here?" she asks carefully, glancing past me at the old, cracked parking lot.

"Yeah, I—" A laugh catches my attention, and I watch as a couple gets out of an SUV, the woman cackling at something he's said. "One second?" The woman nods and I take off across the parking lot at a jog.

"Excuse me!" The couple stops and turns to look at me, the woman's smile wide and a little nervous. As I get closer, I can smell the booze on them, and decide not to comment on the decision to come to an extreme haunt while being at the very least tipsy. "Hey, umm, is this where the haunt is?" I ask, gesturing absently around with one hand.

The guy, who might be a few years older than my twenty-three, nods his head. "Yeah, you're in the right place. It was a bitch to find, right?"

"Right." I turn and give the thumbs up to my understanding driver, who slowly pulls out of the parking lot while her window rolls up slowly. "Seriously, I get why it's so hard to locate but also..." My smile turns apologetic.

"You're not here alone are you?" the girl asks, glancing around like I might have friends waiting to pop out from the cracks in the asphalt. "Who the hell would do an extreme haunt *alone*?"

"Uh, not me." I raise my hands as if in surrender. "My friends are just late." That's a nice way for me to say that Mason and Joey forgot what time we were going to leave and left their phones somewhere other than their bedroom while they acted out Joey's latest bedroom fantasy.

Which, most likely, was only a few keys off of incredibly vanilla.

"Gotcha. Want to walk in with us?" The girl shivers in her lightweight jacket and leans closer to her boyfriend. "I'm Ivy."

"Noa," I reply, glancing back across the parking lot. I want to refuse. I want to stand here and glare as my friends pull up so I can hold it over them that I had to go looking for some viral back alley, underground extreme haunt at eleven pm in a shit part of the city without them.

But my pettiness loses the battle against the eeriness of the parking lot and the cold breeze that's making my teeth chatter a little.

"Yeah, okay." I flash them a smile and fall into step with the two of them. "Is this your first extreme haunt?" I can't help but ask. I can't help but be *curious*.

They glance at each other and Ivy bites her lip, seeming nervous. "It is," she tells me finally as her boyfriend throws an arm over her shoulders. "Dalton found out about it from someone we went to school with. We got lucky and scored tickets before they closed them. It was *crazy* that you had to get an invitation to even sign up, right?"

I roll my shoulders in a shrug. "I didn't get our tickets," I admit. "My friend took care of it and just like, sent me a screenshot I can pull up on my phone."

"Think they'll let you in without the actual thing?" Dalton looks at me, not quite worried. But why would he be? He's not *my* boyfriend.

And judging by the way he's clinging to Ivy and glancing around nervously, I'm pretty okay with that. He seems…jumpy. Nervous. Like he isn't quite sure of this as much as she is. If I was bringing my boyfriend to an extreme haunt, I'd want them to be as enthusiastic to dive into it as I am.

But, then again, I suppose I'd have to get a boyfriend first.

Thinking about his question, I just make a non-committal noise. "Kinda hoping it doesn't come to that. They're just late." As if on cue, my phone vibrates in the pocket of my leggings and I fish it out to look at the screen.

I'm so freaking sorry. The text in the group chat is from Sienna, who is the reason we found this place at all. She's the one obsessed with *Grim Descent* going viral a few years ago, and while I've always been interested in extreme haunts, she's the one who seems to have a fetish for getting one of the prize t-shirts.

If she can make it through to the end, anyway. And I don't have the heart to tell her I've seen her get nervous enough in regular haunted houses that I feel like she won't last five minutes here.

We're so late. God, Noa, we're the worst. We're getting there as fast as we can though, okay? I can tell she's anxious and feels guilty, and I frown at my phone as another typing bubble pops up, this one from Joey.

You got there okay with the Uber?

I wonder if I should tell them the address they gave me hadn't worked in the driver's GPS. If I don't, they'll probably have to drive around like I did until they find the creepy parking lot with the telephone pole ringed in orange lights.

Before I can do more than type a quick *yes* and send it, I collide with a larger figure, yelping softly. "Oh my god, fuck!" I gasp, stumbling back from the person I'd just walked into. "That was so rude of me. I am so sorry I wasn't looking where I was going. I—"

The person turns, surveying me from behind a black mask that looks vaguely like an animal skull. It covers most of his face, with only eye holes for me to judge his expression by. When his mask catches the dim light from outside of the abandoned building, I see it has an upside down red cross carved into it and painted red.

"Oh, damn." Momentarily distracted, I take a step forward toward the silent man, my phone forgotten in my palm even as it vibrates again. "Your mask is so cool." I realize Ivy and Dalton have abandoned me to talk to another couple, but that's okay. I'm not offended, considering I'd been sucked into a text conversation. "Sorry…again. I guess you're in character and won't talk to me, but—"

He lifts a gloved hand and reaches out to tuck my black and orange hair back behind my ear. My stomach does a little flip, and I wonder how realistic it is to want to date a scare actor at an extreme haunt who's hiding his face behind a mask.

With my luck, he's probably fifty-seven and covered in very poorly done tattoos with bad hygiene.

"Sorry," I murmur again, a bit absently. "Umm. By the

way, I'm supposed to be here with my friends, but they're running super late. I have a screenshot of my ticket, but—" He lowers his hand enough to crook two fingers at me, still not talking.

"Okay, well, you are very committed to this no talking thing, huh?" I mutter, swiping out of my text conversation and to my pictures. He leans in close, the scent of his cologne is subtle and spicy in my nose when I inhale sharply.

Fifty-seven and poor hygiene, I remind myself before I can get my hopes up. I've been here before and I've always been disappointed when the mask came off. "Here." With a small, jerky movement, I lift my phone between us until it illuminates his eyes behind the mask.

He definitely has the darkest brown eyes I've ever seen. They look almost black in the stark light of my phone as he narrows them to look over the ticket. "Is this okay? For now? Just until—" He cuts me off with a nod and pushes my phone back toward me with one finger. His gaze finds mine, and the look there is unreadable.

"Thank you," I murmur. I don't know what else to say.

Something about my words makes his eyes narrow shrewdly. Then he tilts his head to the side for just a moment before turning on his heel and prowling across the parking lot toward another actor, this one's wearing a skull mask and staring at me.

Right at me.

My stomach twists and I look away, eyes landing on the group of four that includes Ivy and Dalton. Clearly sensing my distress, the pretty brunette whose name I've known for all of three minutes waves me over, and wastes no time in introducing me to her friends.

"Noa's friends are late," she tells the other couple who've introduced themselves as Alec and Harley. Harley gives me an apologetic half smile, but Alec doesn't even seem to notice me, since he's so wrapped up in his phone.

"They'll be here," I say, waving my own phone dismissively. "Apparently they're..." I glance at the new messages, my heart sinking. "Well, apparently they're about thirty minutes away. Crap." That's...far.

Especially when the heavy door of the warehouse swings open with a loud creaking that makes me grit my teeth, my eyes are drawn toward it automatically.

"Hope they're here soon, or they'll miss it. I don't think they let anyone else in after they start," Ivy murmurs with a sympathetic glance in my direction.

I don't reply, but I watch as another six people filter into the large, open room beyond the door that's well lit and probably warmer than out here. The two couples leave me as well until I'm all alone in the parking lot with just my phone and shivering.

Well, almost alone. The man with the animal skull mask is now standing beside the open door ten or so feet from me, his attention never leaving my face. He glances inside, then back at me, the question clear in the air between us.

"Okay," I sigh. "Yeah, okay. I just...My friends will be here," I tell him, taking a few steps toward the door. "Can I let them in when they get here?"

He doesn't say no or shake his head.

He does *nothing* except watch me. So with a groan, I jog into the warehouse, and the door closes ominously and loudly behind me with a *clang*.

They'd better get here soon. I'm not sure I can do this completely alone. No matter what claims I may have made with the help of cheap, gummy bear vodka.

2

THE CLANG OF THE DOOR ECHOES AROUND THE SOMEWHAT WELL-LIT, sparsely furnished room just inside the door. I stop, glancing around, and forget that Animal Skull has to come in as well. But the knowledge comes back really quick when I feel his fingers on both sides of my waist, pushing me forward a few steps so he can move into the room.

I turn to look at him over my shoulder, eyes wide as I hold his gaze. To my surprise, he doesn't move. He just studies me, looking me over like he's searching for some sign of recognition in my eyes. Like we somehow know each other, but he's trying to figure out where we crossed paths before.

But I've never met anyone with eyes as dark as his. His fingers press against my hip bones, and for half a second he traces along them before he blinks, disinterest clouding over his gaze as he drops his hands and strides to the other side of the room, where the other actors are hanging out. When he stops, it's beside Skeleton Mask, who's once again just *looking* at me.

It makes me feel uneasy, if I'm being truthful.

Suddenly realizing that I'm the only one still standing, I glance toward the wall where the other visitors are sitting in mismatched chairs...only to see that there isn't an extra. Not even a fucking ottoman. That makes me feel weirder, like I don't belong, but I remind myself the whole point of this place is to scare us and make us uncomfortable.

They probably made the chairs too few on purpose, so a few of us would be left standing up and uncomfortable. The other visitors look at me, a few of them noticing the chair situation as well.

Before I can slide down the wall or stand there awkwardly, however, a scraping sound makes me jump.

Skeleton Mask drags a chair over from the other side of the room, all but slamming it down on the ground a small distance from the others. With that done, he just *looks* at me from behind his mask, his light green eyes almost cat-like in their paleness.

When I don't move, he rolls his eyes and beckons me over with a snort. Then, when I'm close enough, he reaches out and drags me into the chair despite my yelp of protest.

You signed up for this, I remind myself silently, hands gripping the arms of the metal chair as I stare up at him with my heart racing nervously.

He's so close I can hear his breathing under the mask.

He's so fucking close that my foot brushes his boot. Without a word he turns, stalking back to his side of the room like a pissed off cat and leaning on the wall next to Animal Skull.

As if that's what they were waiting for, a man in a distorted white mask picks up a remote from a small stool, hitting a button that makes the large tv hanging on one wall turn on. There's a chair on the screen, and the room looks pretty similar to this one, if not the exact same one. Within a few seconds, someone goes to sit in the chair, leaning forward and tapping their heels on the floor impatiently.

Their mask is featureless. Cloth and thick, it and the rest of their black clothing obscures their features entirely.

"Welcome, visitors." The voice is clearly filtered to be unrecognizable, and it doesn't even seem like the masked man is the one doing the talking. He's too busy looking impatient. *"Before we begin, we'll be passing out the waiver for you to sign. Hopefully you've read it over by now and you know what you've signed up for."* The man in the chair leans back until he's looking up at the ceiling, arms resting on the chair limply.

"We will be inviting you back in groups of four maximum. Going in alone is...ill-advised. Your fate may be more bearable if you have someone screaming next to you."

Yeah, my friends really need to show the hell up. I shoot off another text, sitting back in my chair and crossing one leg over the other. My foot bobs nervously in the air, drawing attention to my obvious discomfort as the video goes on.

"After the waivers are looked over and signed, we will begin. If you decide you'd rather leave than finish your experience, all you have to say to our team are the following words..." The man shifts on the chair, the screen going staticky for a few seconds just as distorted words appear on the screen.

FAIR'S FAIR.

A chair creaks and I glance sideways at one of the girls who's looking at the screen like she's seen something that makes her uncomfortable. She glances at her friend, who isn't looking at her, before settling back in her chair nervously.

Curious, I look toward the actors. Most of them are watching the television, except for one girl in a lacy, torn black dress to go with her cracked, porcelain doll mask. Unlike her coworkers, Doll Mask is staring at the group of visitors and tapping her fingers nervously against her thigh. When she notices, the girl beside her in a clown mask taps her hand, watching her until Doll Mask settles back against the wall.

Weird.

But it also probably has nothing to do with me. My attention trails over the other actors, studying their masks and all black outfits. One of the men has on a mask that reminds me of a Roman Emperor, weirdly enough, is dressed in an all black suit, while another is in a black vest and jeans, his arms bare. Skeleton Mask and Animal Skull are both dressed similarly, in outfits that remind me of something tactical or post-apocalyptic scavenger-chic.

Skeleton Mask's outfit has more silver rings on it. His black pants fit a little looser, but they're still tucked into black boots with heavy, thick soles. His tight shirt is pushed up to his elbows, and when he shifts, a line of skin peeks out over his black and silver belt. His hands are covered in gloves as well, with white designs printed over the backs to look like skeletal hands.

As the video goes on to discuss risks, I switch my gaze to Animal Skull, surveying his more subtle outfit. His pants fit a little more snugly, and his shirt is a plain, solid black. His sleeves go all the way to his wrists, where his gloves start. All of it is black and without any accessories.

Except his boots. Sleek black leather climbs his calves, stopping midway toward his knees. The rings where his shoelaces loop through glow gleam bright silver, as does a plate over the heel of the boot and the two buckles interspersed up his leg. I'm pretty sure he must have polished them. None of my boots have ever come out of the box looking anywhere near that good. I also have to assume this is the first time he's worn them, given the shiny perfection of the leather.

Mine are scuffed the moment I lay eyes on them.

Shifting in my chair, I let my gaze travel up his body,

intending on studying the details of his mask before I go back to paying attention to the video.

But my plan falls apart when my gaze finds his, and with a jolt, I realize he's looking at me. Worse still, *he knows I've been staring at him.*

I blink once, feeling heat rise to my face before looking away from him to study the wall. Anything is better than him, and the wall is the easiest thing to stare at.

Though, maybe it wasn't the most subtle move to look away from him like I'm ashamed he caught me. I'm probably going to regret it during the haunt, though I'm not sure exactly how he can use my staring at his boots against me.

Great. This just keeps getting better and better.

The movie's wrapping up, I think, and I look down at my phone that's been silent for the last few minutes. Turning on the screen again, I navigate to our group chat and scroll through the last few messages before sending a quick one of my own.

Where the fuck are you guys? There's no way they're going to make it in time if they don't get here in the next few minutes. And well, maybe not then either.

A touch to my hair has me jumping out of my chair just as Roman Emperor starts handing out waivers on clipboards with pens. I glance up, eyes wide, to find Doll Mask stroking my hair almost affectionately.

"Pretty," she breathes softly, too quietly for anyone else to hear, as she drags her fingers down the black and orange strands. "Just so...*pretty.*"

"Let's, uh, not oversell." I chuckle softly, nervous as hell. "No offense to myself, but I know there are way prettier girls in this room. Probably you, too." Not that I know, but her whole outfit really exudes a gothic kind of beauty.

Her fingers pause in my hair and she steps closer, almost

seeming unsure. She glances up, just as Roman Emperor stops in front of me with nothing in his hands. "We seem to have run out of waivers. Someone brought an extra guest," he tells me in a flat voice.

Doll Mask starts stroking my hair again, and I try not to duck away or do anything she might find hurtful.

Though I'm not sure why the hell I care about someone else's *feelings* in an extreme haunt meant to break me. My feelings are probably much more at risk than hers tonight. But she just continues to pet me like a dog or a nervous child.

I'm not sure which I'd rather be, honestly.

"Umm...Okay. Do you need me to...?" My heart thumps nervously, and I try to swallow down my anxiety as Roman Emperor looks at Doll Mask.

I'm not expecting him to take a step closer to me. I *definitely* don't expect him to lean down, his mask only inches from my face. The movement makes me yelp softly in surprise; I'd jerk back, but Doll Mask's hand doesn't let me.

"We can't legally enforce our rules without a signed waiver," he whispers, his eyes catching and holding mine. "But you are also free to walk out of here, since you won't have the binding legality of its protection if we...go too far. So what do you say, friend?"

The room seems both incredibly loud and incredibly small as I stare at him, processing his words. *Go too far* is a terrifying statement. Even though some part of me says he's not telling the truth.

"I'll...stay. If I'm allowed," I breathe, unable to look away. "I want to stay."

He stands up at my words and glances back to the other side of the room, head tilting toward me. When I follow his gaze, Animal Skull pushes off the wall, heading to a door in the back of the room and disappearing behind it.

"All right then." Roman Emperor looks back down at me, amusement and interest clear in his eyes. As he studies me, Doll Mask's movements pick up, her petting of my hair becoming a little bit painful as she tugs on the orange ends. "What's your name?"

"Noa," I reply. "Noa Torrance."

He trades a look with Doll Mask, who nods.

"Then you're here to stay, Noa Torrance."

3

By the time everyone else has signed and handed in their wavers, I've texted my friends approximately sixteen times back to back with no reply.

I'm starting to think they were murdered, quite honestly. Biting my lip, I sit back in my chair, wishing it didn't creak so much. My breath leaves me in a low sigh when the actors once again line up on the other side of the room, all of them looking so strangely *formal*.

It's like they're here for some kind of planned, choreographed event that has more meaning to it than just a viral underground haunted house on Halloween night. My eyes flick over all of them again, but this time I don't stare at anyone in particular.

"Welcome, friends." Roman Emperor sweeps out his arms in front of himself and from the corner of my eye I watch Skeleton Mask prowl over to stand in front of the door leading back out to the parking lot. "We're so lucky you've agreed to join us here tonight."

A murmur of excitement goes through the others, and I see Ivy lean into her boyfriend and grip his arm.

"Let me introduce your guides and hosts for this evening, shall I?" He steps forward, gesturing first at the girl with the doll mask. "Hex. Blight." He gestures at the girl in the clown mask and works his way down the line until he gets to the end where Skeleton Mask and Animal Skull stand. "Ravage." He points at Skeleton mask, then at Animal Skull. "And our handsome Harrow."

The animal mask tilts to the side, studying Roman Emperor.

"And I'll be here to get you whatever you need. You may call me *Nero*." He sweeps a bow, and my eyes narrow.

Does he know exactly what that name means? Or rather, the story of the emperor who made it famous? It seems...ill-fated. Though I suppose most people who *didn't* have three Roman history classes in college might not know who Nero was.

Or what he did.

"We've decided the order for tonight's fun. If you'll indulge my friend here and let him sort you into groups?" Another man steps forward, and as I watch, he starts to move the other visitors into groups, using gestures and touch more than his words. If he even speaks at all.

When I look back, I notice most of the actors have left the room, the door to the black hallway behind Nero is open as Doll Mask skips through it.

By the time everyone is grouped up, it's pretty clear I'm still alone. My stomach twists, and I cross my legs nervously, foot bobbing in the air once more and giving away that I'm anxious.

But then again, I'm sure everyone here is anxious. Even the ones who are pretending to be completely unbothered.

My vision is obscured by a black figure, and when I look up

I find Skeleton Mask staring at me, fingers tapping against his arm.

"It was...Ravage, right?" I ask, watching him as he just *stands there*. He nods once, but doesn't say or do anything else.

"And the guy in the animal skull, that's Harrow?" They aren't exactly words I use on a daily basis, and Nero went through the names pretty fast.

This time I don't get a nod in reply. At least not right away. Ravage watches me until my phone lights up in my hands and draws my eyes down to it.

And his too, judging by the way he kneels down, rocking forward on his heels to peer at my phone as well. "Well, you're certainly welcome to message them back," I mutter with surprise, theatrically holding up my phone to the masked man.

Unexpectedly, he takes it out of my hand, plucking it from my palm with his skeletal gloves and turning it so he can read the texts, too.

I watch him scroll through the conversation, and finally his eyes find mine through the eyeholes of his mask. Slowly he tips his head to one side, then the other, before tugging off his glove to type out a message on my phone, hit send, and hand it back to me.

But not before his fingers brush against mine, a movement that makes my little, hopeless romantic heart twist in excitement. My eyes fall to the message he's sent in response to my friends' promises that they're about to pull into the parking lot.

YOU'LL BE TOO LATE.

The message makes me glance up at him, and I swear I can see the flicker of excitement in his eyes. "That's a little dramatic," I murmur. "Don't you think?"

This time I *know* I hear his chuckle. He rocks forward onto the balls of his feet, pressing one hand to my knee. It seems like he wants to say something until a gloved hand descends on his shoulder and both of us look up into Harrow's animal skull mask.

He's not looking at me this time, however. His attention is all for Ravage as he tugs him to his feet with a small shake of his head. I shift nervously, which unfortunately prompts them both to look at me silently from behind their imposing masks.

My phone vibrates in my hands, but I don't look away from the intimidating pair. I don't think I *can*, truthfully.

"So...*Texas Chainsaw Massacre* is my favorite movie," I say conversationally, unable to give into rambling from nervousness. "And I mean that as in, like, all movies, not just horror movies. The classic, obviously, but the remakes are fine. Except the new one, which—" A quick roll of Harrow's eyes is the only warning I get before he's covering my mouth with his hand, forcing my words to come to a halt.

Which is more than fine, really, since they really were just me rambling away my anxieties at them.

His gloved thumb strokes along my lower lip as I watch them both and squirm under their gazes. Finally, I have to pull away, and I drag my lower lip into my mouth to bite it nervously. Then, without a word, they just turn and walk away as if triggered by some unspoken signal I certainly didn't catch.

Eventually, my eyes fall back to my phone, and I scroll through the few messages I've gotten in the last minute or so. My friends are predictably weirded out by my last message, though I'm not about to tell them a guy in a mask sent it instead of me.

You just need to hurry the fuck up. I'm not sure what I'll do if they don't get here in time. Really, I'm not sure what I *can* do, other than apologize and call an Uber. I suppose, according to Nero, there are more people here than they'd expected, so they probably won't mind if my friends don't show up and—

A scream sounds from further inside the warehouse, prompting my phone to clatter to the floor when my hands jerk in surprise. I murmur a soft curse and pick it up, feeling around the device for any cracks or scuffs. Thankfully, it survived the fall without a blemish. Which is more than can be said for my last four phones.

May they all rest in pieces.

"It's part of the haunt, you baby," whispering the words to myself, I shift to try to find some comfort in the chair I'm sitting in. A quick count shows me two of the four groups have already been taken back, and two more groups, one of two and one of three individuals, are the only ones left. Ivy and Dalton are the pair, and Ivy smiles at me anxiously, unable to stand still now that she's next in line.

All I do is give her a little mock salute before looking down at my phone again.

We're here, so where are you?

Relief floods me, making me feel like my ribs are no longer trying to press my heart to pieces. Thank fucking God they're here so I won't be alone anymore.

Inside. The door's shut, I'll ask them to open it.

Glancing up, I watch as Ivy and her boyfriend are beckoned down the hallway, leaving only me and a group of three college-aged boys. They joke and tease each other, one of them catching my eye and wiggling his brows suggestively.

The movement makes my nose scrunch, but I don't have a chance to make some childish and rude gesture back. Ravage is suddenly there, reaching out to slam his hand into the wall by the guy's head and leaning in close.

The guy yelps and jerks back, nearly cracking his head on the wall before glaring up at the masked man and muttering something at him that probably isn't friendly.

But Ravage doesn't react. Instead, he turns to look at me, head tilting as if asking for my opinion or advice.

Like he wants *me* to decide if he should let the guy off the wall.

My phone rings, dragging my attention down to it, and when I see Sienna's name on the screen, I bring it to my ear, huffing out a sigh. "Can you, like, come to the door?" I ask in a soft whisper.

"*What fucking door, Noa?*" Sienna sounds exasperated as hell, and I hear other voices in the background. "*We talked to the staff to see where you are, but they're saying you're not here.*"

"I'm definitely fucking here—" Another scream cuts me off and I glance up to see the three boys filing down the hallway, still joking and laughing. "Maybe *you're* not here. Do you see the door to the building?"

"*Yeah. It's closed, but are you sure that's where you are? I haven't seen anyone go in or out.*" She sounds unsure, and maybe even a little disbelieving.

"You think I'm lying to you about where I am? Sienna, you're late. They've already done the waiver signing and everything." Looking up again, I find that I'm alone in the room.

Except for Harrow.

He stands in front of the closed door to the hallway while two screams ring out. His attention is fully trained on me, and that's when it hits me I really am *alone*.

"You're really gonna miss it if you don't hurry up." I'm distracted, sure, but I'm really just desperate for my friends to get in here. But since they're here, I push to my feet and warily approach the only other person in the room. "My friends say they're outside," I tell him, my words a little quieter than I intend. "Can I go and look for them?"

Slowly, he shakes his head and lifts one finger to tap his wrist, like he's telling me the time.

Like he's telling me it's too late for them to get in. "Sienna, I don't think he's going to let you guys in. You are seriously *so late* and—" Harrow reaches out, his fingers crooking toward me for my phone. In response, I glance back at the door I came in through, biting my lip.

"*Are you sure we're in the same place?*" Sienna's starting to sound even more unsure of the situation, and I can hear Joey asking if everything's okay. "*Can you come outside? Show us where to go?*"

Hearing her, Harrow shakes his head slowly and his fingers twitch again. "No, I...I gotta go. I hate that you're not here and God, I'm probably going to safeword out so fast, but I don't want to miss this when it's never going to happen for us again. I'll call you later, okay?" Hanging up the phone on her protests, I drop my hand to my side and stare at the man in front of me.

Yet again, he crooks his fucking fingers at me.

"You want...?" I glance down at my phone, surprised, and look back up at him. He nods once, just as my phone starts vibrating incessantly. Even when I hit the button for it to go to voicemail, Sienna just calls me back once more.

"I'll get it back in one piece, right?" I ask, waiting for him to nod before adding. "And all I have to do for it to stop is say Fair's Fair?"

There's a little hesitation, but Harrow steps forward and meets my gaze, his eyes so impossibly dark, and nods.

A low huff leaves me and I reach up, pressing my phone into his hand and hoping I'm not getting into something that's going to give me trauma for the rest of my life.

4

The door clanging shut behind me feels so...final. I turn to look over my shoulder in time to see Harrow lean back against it, his mask seeming to taunt me in the dim hallway.

"Am I..." I don't even know what I want to ask. But he doesn't move, only watches me, and it almost seems like he's patiently waiting for me to ask my question.

A scream makes me glance forward, but I look back at him for some kind of reassurance that he definitely isn't about to give. Sure enough, he just fucking stands there. "I know you aren't going to say anything to make me feel better...or at all." Sighing, my foot scuffs on the floor, and I find myself shivering even in my hoodie and fleece-lined leggings. "I'm just rambling, okay?"

He still just stands there.

"Okay, okay." I suck in a breath. "Do I just...walk? That way?" Again I shiver, this time my teeth chattering a little just in time to hear the sound of a revving chainsaw. "Wow, I hate chainsaws." It's probably the wrong thing to say, since this is a haunt designed to absolutely destroy me.

I swear I hear him give a soft huff from behind his mask. Turning, I find Harrow pushing away from the wall to stalk closer to me, one hand raised and reaching toward me. Instead of pushing me back or spinning me around, his long fingers wrap around my throat tightly enough for my breath to catch in my throat. I reach up, fingers hovering over his wrist. I don't think I'm really allowed to touch him back, after all.

He pushes me, forcing me to walk backwards down the dim hallway at a pace that makes it somewhat easy for me not to trip. His thumb moves as we walk, stroking along my jaw in a way that makes my stomach twist with something that isn't at all fear.

"Sorry," I murmur, not sure what I'm even apologizing for. But for some reason Harrow stops, studying me from behind his mask as he strokes over my jaw again before letting go and dropping his hand.

For just a few seconds, everything in the warehouse is silent. Nothing moves around us, and the sounds of screams and whatever else have fallen away in a lull. As he stares at me, I swear he's going to say *something*. Especially when he lifts his hand again, only to drop it with a shake of his head.

It's...confusing, to say the least. Harrow brushes past me, banging on the closed door at the end of the hall, making the metal clang as the sound echoes through the enclosed space. I can't help my wince at the sudden, sharp noise, and as I watch, the door swings open to reveal Doll Mask, whose fake alias I don't remember.

When she sees me, she goes up on her toes, excitement in every line of her body. She's spattered with what I hope is fake blood, but as she takes a step toward me, Harrow reaches out quickly to grab her arm and pull her to a stop.

She glances at him, shying back like she's afraid of him, but he steps closer and leans in, their masks so close I'm surprised they don't touch. Whether he says something or not is lost on me as another scream echoes through the warehouse.

When it's over, they're both looking at me. Harrow releases her arm and steps back, standing by the open door and leaning his weight on it to keep it from closing. But this time, he doesn't stop her from skipping toward me, arms outstretched like she's been waiting to see me.

I cringe away from her, expecting the worst, but she only wraps me up in her arms, having to stand on her toes to be face-to-face with me. "*Pretty*," she breathes softly, her eyes barely visible behind the mask. She holds my gaze, her fingers gripping my hoodie and pulling me forward as she dances backward.

"All I have to do is safeword, right?" I breathe, heart thumping in my chest as she pulls me towards the open door. She doesn't answer, instead glancing over her shoulder at Harrow, a question in her movement.

He's the one to nod once, head dipping in assent at my question, so I take a breath and stop resisting her, instead letting her pull me through the open door completely at her leisure.

And on this side, the door is just as loud as it slams closed behind me, making me jump and causing Doll Mask to giggle in my ear. "So jumpy, aren't you?" Her fingers twine with mine. "You're just so easy." She sounds so pleased with herself. Like she's done something to be proud of that she can't get over and wants the whole world to see.

In a way, she reminds me of a cat presenting their owner with a dead mouse.

"I'm not trying to be," I admit, twining my fingers with hers in return. The action seems to shock her, judging by the way she looks down at our hands for a few seconds. But then she shakes her head and looks at me again, her black dress stiff in some places with what looks like dried blood.

"We'll go see Banshee first." The way she says it is conversational. "She does such creative things in her room." She swings her arm, gripping my hand so I'm forced to swing mine as well as I walk side-by-side with her down a hallway with multiple doors lining either side. It's maybe not quite what I was expecting, but dread makes my stomach twist when she stops in front of a pink door.

Demurely, Doll Mask knocks, waiting for something I can't hear before twisting the handle and opening the door to the room beyond it.

Lights assault my eyes instantly, causing me to blink away the spots that dance in my vision after going from the dark hallway to the brightly lit…circus tent?

That's what it looks like, anyway. But it takes a few seconds for my brain to recognize what I'm seeing, and I lock my teeth together tight to remind myself this isn't real.

None of this is real. But the point is to make me think it is, so as long as I keep reminding myself of that, I might actually last five minutes in here.

A wheel spins lazily against the far wall, and from it hangs the most realistic looking fake body I've ever seen. Knives stick out of the man's body, pinning his hands and feet to it and sticking out of his abdomen like a pincushion. There's a bag over the man's head, preventing me from seeing what his face looks like, and when Doll Mask tugs on my hand, I turn to look at her, not as freaked out as I was expecting.

Until I see the other girl, who's wearing a clown mask, sitting on top of a plastic picnic table. She runs her fingers over the circular saw in her lap, covered in blood from head to toe. When I gasp, she looks up at me, hopping off the table to prowl toward me with the saw.

"You're so lost," she murmurs when she's close enough. "Here." She grabs my free hand and rests the blade of the circular saw against my palm, not letting me pull away as she slides the bloody flat of the blade against my skin. "Is it still warm? Everything's always so cold to me."

"No," I whisper, eyes on the blood as carnival music plays softly in the background. My hand shakes as she strokes the edge of the blade along it, and I can't help noticing just how keenly Doll Mask watches her do it.

"Don't cut her," my companion murmurs. "Don't mix their blood."

Clown Girl glances her way with a quiet scoff and lets go of my hand so I can drop it back to my side. "I'm not like Blight." Her voice is thick with scorn. "I won't break your pretty friend. Come here." She reaches out, tangling her fingers in the strings of my hoodie and dragging me across the room. "Look at what I did. *Look how pretty they are.*"

Against the far wall, two more bodies are slumped on the floor. They're very clearly dead, or faking it more likely, with their heads covered by clown masks and blood pouring from the eyeholes that are pierced by long metal skewers. Clown Girl kneels down beside them and drags me down with her until my knees hit the concrete floor and something wet soaks into the fabric.

It's not real blood, I tell myself, repeating the sentiment over and over again. *It's so not real blood.* That's what I have to remember about this.

Doll Mask kneels behind me, arms wrapped around my shoulders as she watches Clown Girl reach forward, her fingers teasing at the end of a skewer. "Would you like one?" she asks offhandedly, and before I can tell her no fucking thank you, she rips the metal stick out of the clown mask, the bloody end of it nearly turning my stomach.

I lurch backward into Doll Mask, who giggles and holds me relatively still. Blood and viscera drip from the end of the skewer, where the remains of the fake eye dangles precariously. God, it looks so...*real.*

"It's not real," I tell myself in a whisper as Clown Girl holds the skewer closer to my face. "Fuck, that looks so real." Not that I know what my eye would look like in this...condition.

"It isn't? We'll have to tell her that." Clown Girl sidles closer to the masked body and reaches out to tap her shoulder. "Hey, Hannah?" she hums. "Your eye isn't real. *Noa* said so." Her use of my name makes me shiver, and I try to stand up only to be held down by Doll Mask. "So you're okay with me taking it, right? Actually..."

She stands up and Doll Mask drags me up as well. "Why don't you take it, Noa?" she chirps.

"No, I don't...That's okay," I reply as my heart races nervously in my chest. "I think maybe you should keep it."

"I have three more. Five more, if I want to take his." She looks at the wheel and reaches out to grab my wrist, her bloody hand sliding over my skin and leaving a red swipe behind. "I said take it, didn't I?" she asks, forcing my fingers to close over the end of the skewer where the fake eye is, even as I yelp in protest.

But I can't stop her from making me crush it between my fingers, the fake eye squishing like jelly and seeping out from between my knuckles in a way that makes me want to puke. The moment she lets go, I jerk back, staring down at my hand in revulsion while Doll Mask just giggles and rests her head against my arm. "This is so gross," I whisper, shaking my hand and causing the viscera to spatter against the floor. Looking around, I look for anything to wipe my hand on, even as Doll Mask tugs me back toward the door.

"She likes to have alone time after," the girl whispers in my ear while I surreptitiously wipe my hand on the fabric covered wall. "She'll get mad if we don't leave her alone."

"Oh, you won't get an argument out of me," I assure her with a forced, nervous smile. Honestly, as gross as the fake eye on the skewer was, it feels…tame. I'd expected to be hauled around or tied up. Hell, I'd even prepared myself for waterboarding.

Relief uncurls in my chest as Doll Mask pulls me out of the room and down the hallway. It occurs to me that if this is going to be more me looking at things and having to put gross shit in my hand…and circular saws…maybe I can do this after all.

"If you want to keep her"—Clown Girl's voice rings out down the hallway and I turn to see her leaning on the bright door of her room, mask tilted in our direction—"take her somewhere Rav won't find her."

It's just part of the act, I remind myself again as Doll Mask glances back at her coworker. She gives a small nod and turns to another door, this one a pristine white…except for the blood smeared over the surface near the knob.

"Let's play," she whispers, and drags me inside as my stomach twists and I ask myself why the hell I did this to myself.

Especially on my own.

The room is remarkably less overwhelming than the circus tent. I'm surprised to find I'm in a child's bedroom, or what looks like one, with a wrought iron bed in one corner and a table holding a dollhouse in the middle as the main feature of the room. A light bulb flickers above us, and when Doll Mask tugs me further into the room, I nearly stumble when my sneakers sink into the soaking wet carpet.

Looking down is a bit of a mistake, though. I bite my lip to stifle a gasp when I see blood bubbling to the surface of the plush fabric, streaking along my sneakers. I follow the puddles of blood, seeing that they end near the bed.

I'm not sure I want to know why.

"Come see." Doll Mask doesn't give me much of a choice. She drags me over to the dollhouse, showing me the side that opens, which immediately makes me gasp in surprise.

It's covered in blood, and what looks like entrails are draped garishly over it like streamers or fairy lights. But my new friend doesn't even hesitate. She picks up a string of gore, running it between her dainty fingers before holding it out to me.

"N-no, I—" She doesn't give me a choice. She reaches out, looping the stringy mass around my wrist, her hands slipping in blood as she tries to tie them in a bow to form a little bracelet.

It's not real.

The warm, slick slide against my skin turns my stomach. It's so hard to remember none of this is real when another scream rings through the building, and both of us look toward the door.

"Ooh, I didn't realize she was still alive," Doll Mask comments. "Let's go see." She grabs my fingers in hers, skin slick with blood, and tugs me to the door. Subtly I pick at the 'bracelet,' dropping it to the floor with a shudder.

Not that Doll Mask even stops to notice. She heads for a black door and pushes it open, dragging me inside as I brace myself for something just as bad as the last two rooms.

But what I get is so, so much worse.

Dalton sits in a chair in the middle of the room, covered in blood and sobbing. When he sees me his eyes go wide, and he struggles in the chair where his arms are cuffed to the rails beside him. "Help me!" he screams, rattling the cuffs. "This isn't fucking fake! *Help me!*"

Dread settles in my chest and I look at the man behind him, the one in the scarecrow mask. He stares back at me impassively, then leans down to pick up a chainsaw from the concrete floor.

Fuck, I hate chainsaws in haunted houses.

"Help me!" Dalton screams again, unable to see what Scarecrow is doing. "It's not—These guys are fucking insane! Ivy's dead, and—" The chainsaw revs and he stiffens, a look of pure terror going through his eyes.

"S-so safeword out," I stammer, unable to take my eyes off of the chainsaw. "Just say—"

"I fucking tried! Fair's fair! Fair is *fucking fair!*" He's hysterical with fear and panic, and I glance between the two actors, expecting them to stop, to untie him. To do...something.

But Scarecrow just revs the chainsaw again, despite Dalton's screams of protest. With Doll Mask's hand tightly holding mine, I can't even look away as Scarecrow strides forward. He reaches out, stroking bloody fingers along Dalton's face, and leans in to whisper something to him I have no chance of hearing.

Whatever it is, though, has the man in the chair looking floored, disbelief in his eyes as he turns his head to look at the masked man. "No, I...how do you..." he trails off. "It's not my fucking fault!" he sneers, struggling with renewed urgency. "It's not my fault!"

He screams the words as Scarecrow pulls the string on the chainsaw, starting it effortlessly. I stare at it, watching it vibrate in his hand as my heart tries to escape the cage of my ribs by any means possible, making my chest ache with the ferocity of its pulse.

"Fair's fair," I whisper, unable to tear my eyes away. I watch as the chainsaw comes down and makes contact with Dalton's outstretched left arm just below his elbow.

"Fair's fair," I breathe again, as the chainsaw presses *down, down*...the revving of the motor unable to completely drown out Dalton's screaming.

I've never heard someone scream like that before, or seen blood spray and arc while someone tries to rip free. I can see the cuff on his other hand cutting into the skin of his wrist as he tries in desperation to break out of the chair.

I fucking *watch* when the chainsaw sparks against the metal of the chair, severing Dalton's arm and making him slump back in the chair. His forearm is still cuffed to the chair, but falls to hang by the wrist, almost touching the floor.

That's what does it, for some reason. The sight of his arm just *hanging* there, like a prop, while blood sprays from his elbow, has me ripping my hand free of Doll Mask and turning to sprint to the door. I can't do this. It looks too real, and I absolutely have to get out of here. My hand goes for the doorknob, and it takes me a few seconds longer than it should to rip it open to the hallway beyond.

Only I find my path blocked by the man in the skeleton mask. Ravage. I remember his 'name,' after the impression he'd made out in the lobby.

"Fair's fair!" I gasp, panicked as he just leans against the doorframe as casually as if we're about to discuss the weather. "I-I can't do this. I want out, and—"

"You want out?" He reaches up, fingers wrapping around my throat to drag me closer until I can see the glint of his eyes in the dim light. "Princess, where do you think you *are*?"

"I'm..." I start to look over my shoulder, until I hear the revving of the chainsaw again, along with another choked off scream from Dalton. "We're at Grim Descent. The extreme haunt." My words come out almost like a question, and I hate the way his eyes narrow in amusement.

"*Are* we? Are you *sure* that's where you are?" He drags me closer, forcing me to stumble over my own feet until my body is only inches from his. "Or did you maybe end up somewhere you shouldn't, in a game you weren't invited to?"

"But…"

"Maybe it wasn't your friends who were in the wrong place, Noa." I can hear the excitement in his voice, along with something darker that fills me with dread.

"Maybe you wandered somewhere that you shouldn't have, and now you don't get to wander back out."

5

The few seconds of his fingers flexing around my throat while Dalton screams drag out for an eternity. It's so hard to pull in a breath, even though he's not really putting pressure on my neck, and I shudder when I hear the sound of the chainsaw cutting through flesh once again.

"You should look," Ravage murmurs, leaning in close. "It's so much better if you look." Without giving me a choice, he crowds closer to me, wrapping an arm around my shoulders to force me to turn around.

Dalton is no longer screaming. Part of me hopes he's not awake, only slumped in the chair as he is with his severed arms dripping blood to pool on the floor below. I bite my lip hard; the pain is stinging and sharp, and a low sound escapes my lips at the sight.

"He had it coming," Ravage croons, pressing his mask to my face. "Don't feel bad for him when he absolutely…" he keeps talking, telling me all about the things that should've happened, that will happen to Dalton before he's really dead, but I'm not paying attention.

I *can't* pay attention.

Doll Mask holds my gaze, seemingly unnoticed by the two other masked men in the room. As I watch, she tilts her head to one side, turning to look at something close to me. So I look too, finding a small table full of bloody tools and pieces of... something I don't want to identify.

And close to my fingers is a knife. A small switchblade that's still open, mostly clean and just sitting there invitingly. I'm *so close* to it, I really could just reach out and...

When I look back at Doll Mask, she nods her head at me subtly, barely noticeable at all while the man with the chainsaw says something to Ravage.

But I'm terrified. Fucking *terrified* that if I fuck this up, that switchblade will go straight in my chest and I'll be the one in the chair about to get her arms sawed off. On the other hand...

My eyes drift back to Dalton, whose eyes are open now and staring dully in my direction. That's what makes up my mind. I cannot, I *will not* let that be me. Not while I can still do something about it, anyway. Before I can stop myself, I grab the switchblade and whirl into Ravage's hold, lifting it to plunge down into his chest.

He's faster than I expect and he manages to shove away my hand. The shift is just enough that instead of stabbing him, the blade cuts into his arm, deep enough to make him spit a curse but probably not doing any real damage.

At least I keep the knife as he stumbles back. "You *bitch*," he sneers, a laugh in his words as he grips his bleeding upper arm. "Oh, princess..." His words end in a low, threatening growl and he lunges for me, giving me a small opening to lurch past him into the hallway.

Turning, I grab the door, catching sight of Doll Mask from the corner of my eye as she gently holds onto Scarecrow's wrist. Neither of them is trying to come after me, and a flicker of relief travels through my chest.

When Ravage moves to follow me, I slam the door shut, he collides with the heavy wood before I manage to close it all the way. I hear his snarl of outrage, and a clatter that I hope means he stabbed himself on every sharp implement sitting on the table. Then I turn and flee down the hallway, hoping I'm heading for the right end of it that'll take me back to the lobby and ultimately the parking lot.

God, I wish I had my phone.

I barge through the door at the end of the hall, grateful that I made the right decision and ended up back in the empty hallway. Without hesitating, I run to the far door, my blood-covered hands slipping around the handle.

This isn't fake.

I try to turn it, to unlock it, but I realize quickly I'm locked in. Hell, I don't even know where to begin to look for the keys to this place, and when I hear a yell from the hallway behind me, I decide I can't stand here and try to wish the door open anymore.

"Fuck," I hiss, heading to the other door in the lobby. It's on a different wall than the hallway door, and thankfully, it's unlocked.

But even as I sprint through the dark room on the other side of it, I still can't get the thought out of my head that this *isn't fake.*

The eye was real.

The bracelet of gore was real.

The chainsaw cutting through Dalton's arms was fucking real.

My breathing comes in sharp, uneven pants as I stumble through the poorly lit warehouse, trying not to trip over the construction equipment and furniture that litter the space. A few times I fail, stumbling over pieces of something or scattered lumber with soft curses.

When the door to the lobby slams back against the wall on its hinges, light pours into the warehouse behind me. I turn, seeing Ravage stalk inside before he closes the door, plunging us into darkness again.

"Princess..." he calls, his purr echoing in the room. "Are we playing hide-and-seek?" I hear his steps echo on the concrete floor, and I duck under a large table, eyes fixed on his silhouette and the knife gripped tightly in my fingers. Too tightly, judging by how much they ache around the hilt of the blade.

"This is so kind of you, so thoughtful. It's my favorite game, and I know all the hiding spots in here." I can barely see him as he drifts deeper into the room, but I hear him rummaging around, knocking things over in his search for me. "Did I mention that the only way out is through the lobby door? And that without the key that's in my pocket, you're stuck in here?" He sounds way too happy when he says it, and I bite my lip to fight the urge to roll my eyes at his arrogance.

This definitely isn't the time for my disdain.

Hearing his footsteps looming closer, it occurs to me that this is a shitty hiding place. Even with the lights off, the moonlight filtering in the high windows lends enough illumination that he'll probably be able to see me, if he's really looking.

And judging by how thoroughly he's going through the place, he's really fucking looking. Slowly, I edge backwards, dropping to my knees to crawl out from under the table the other way. Somehow I manage to do it without making a sound, and I make my way silently toward the piles of plywood behind me. It's not perfect, but nothing here is perfect.

The gap between two of the pieces that lean against the wall is just big enough for me to squeeze into, and I back in carefully, barely making a sound as the wood shifts ever so slightly.

"Would you like to know what I intend to do with you when I find you?" His voice is closer now, way too close, and I flinch, flexing my fingers around the knife as they start to cramp. "If we're being honest...I haven't quite decided yet. Not the whole game, anyway. I just know I'm aching to play with you. See..." I hear him knock over something else in his search for me, but I don't move.

"I didn't have any guests to play with tonight. I guess I went a little overboard last year, and no one was worth my time this Halloween. Until you walked in, anyway. It doesn't follow the rules, but"—he chuckles—"we gave you every single chance to leave. We made it *so clear* you came to the wrong place. Grim Descent?" He snorts. "Babe, how the hell do you get this lost when their parking lot is the most obvious thing in the world?"

I roll my eyes at his continued monologue, making a face. He really is making this worse than it needs to be, and I wonder if he ever shuts up. Clearly he enjoys the sound of his own voice; though if I wasn't sure he was about to kill me very slowly and very painfully, I probably would, too.

"That's okay, though. I can't even be mad at you. Do you know why?" His soft voice is way too close, and as his steps scuff against the cement, I hold my breath and pray he doesn't look here.

Suddenly the sheets of plywood over me are yanked away, crashing to the floor moments before a hand closes around my throat. "Because if you were where you were supposed to be, I wouldn't have anyone to play with," Ravage snarls in my ear.

"No!" I fumble with the knife, but this time he's ready for me. His other hand grips mine, keeping it away from him as he drags me back across the room far enough that my hip slams into the large wooden table I'd been hiding under. I yelp in surprise and pain, writhing in his grip and wrestling for control of the knife.

"I don't want to play with you!" I shriek, close enough to his mask that my lips brush the latex of it.

He snarls out an unfriendly laugh in response. "Too damn bad, Noa. But I'll tell you what. Give me the knife, and it'll sway me into being a little nicer to you. Come on. Be my good fucking princess and *give me the knife*."

My only response is to scream at him, the words *fuck* and *you* in the sound somewhere. I tighten my grip on the blade instead, and slam his hand into the table harshly, forcing the blade to cut into his palm.

His answering yell is sharp and feral, more like a howl than anything else, and his grip on my neck shifts until his fingers are wrapped around the front of my throat. "Oh, I'm so sorry," he sneers in my face. "I didn't know you wanted to play rough. I'll give you what you want. All you had to do was ask." His fingers tighten, my empty hand coming up to sink my nails into his forearm.

"Don't," I gasp, eyes wide. "Stop! I can't—"

"*Breathe?*" He laughs darkly. "Yeah, that's the point. Or have you never done a little breath play before? Have you never let someone choke you out while they fuck your pretty pussy, Noa?"

My stomach flips at the words, and I jerk backward, only succeeding in hitting my thighs painfully on the table again.

"No?" he continues, not seeming to mind his blood that slicks my palm. "You haven't? Are you telling me I'll be the first to make your vision go all blurry while I fuck you? Oh princess, you'll have to tell me all about coming when you're on the verge of passing out...if I don't go too far. I'm not always so good at control." His fingers flex around my throat, and when he presses down again, the pain is different. Sharper, warmer, and almost immediately spots swim in my vision.

"There it is," Ravage purrs. "That's the sweet spot, isn't it?" All I can do is whimper, my fingers trembling around his wrist and around the knife. I sob in protest, eyes closing hard, but his only reply is a soft snarl in my ear. "Are you going to let go, or am I going to have to choke you into unconsciousness?"

"That one." The words come out a breathy gasp, and I open my eyes to glare at him, only to see a look of surprise in his bright green gaze.

"Oh Noa..." he purrs finally, a rueful chuckle in his words. "Oh, you'd really better be careful or I'm going to get attached. Now let me ask you one more time, okay? I'll even do this..." He loosens his grip just enough that I can take an uninhibited breath, and my lungs burn with relief when I gasp. My eyes close hard as I pull in another drag of oxygen, my breathing the only sound in the warehouse.

"There you go. Breathe, babe. You're all good." His thumb strokes the side of my throat, trailing along my jaw. "Now I'll ask you nicely one more time, okay?" His mask slides against my face, making me shudder. "Won't you pretty please give me the knife, Noa? Before you hurt yourself with it?"

He waits. So fucking patiently, it's irritating while I pant harshly. He doesn't even mind my fingers still digging into his wrist. Ravage just stands there, pinning me to the table behind me.

"I..." I take a breath and my heart twists painfully as I realize what I'm about to do. But I can't let go of the knife. *I can't.*

Not willingly, anyway. If I do and he kills me, then I'll regret it for the few seconds or minutes or hours that it takes for me to die.

I can't give up the only weapon I have against him.

"Not in a million—" When I don't even get to finish the sentence, it dawns on me that Ravage was expecting me to say no, considering the way his hand is quick to close around my throat once more. He lets go of my hand with the knife too fast and unexpectedly for me to take advantage of it, and grabs the front of my hoodie to haul me off my feet before slamming me down on the heavy, sturdy table I'd hidden under.

The movement knocks the air out of me, and it's way too easy for him to reach out and snatch the knife from my hand without much fight.

"That's okay." Without pulling his fingers from my neck, he hops up onto the table, moving to straddle my hips. My hands come up to push against him, fear filling my lungs in the place of oxygen as I cry out in protest. "I didn't want to do it the easy way, either. I get it, princess." Still holding me down with just one hand, he lifts the knife to gaze at it. "I'm not even sure who this belongs to," he admits conversationally as my nails dig into his forearm. His fingers shift against my throat, finding that place again, and I whimper in fear and terrified anticipation.

"Shhh, *shh*. I'm just holding you here. You're fine." But he lowers the knife, returning his attention to me, and gently taps the tip of the blade against my nose. "I can't believe you actually cut me, truthfully. I didn't think you had it in you. You're such a feral little thing when you're cornered, aren't you?" His voice is soft, silky, and filled with sickly sweet kindness.

"Let me go," I gasp, heels pressed against the table as I try to get the leverage to push him off. "You said I wasn't invited— I'm not supposed to be here. So just let me leave, *please*." I'm not above begging, apparently. "I won't tell anyone. I promise I won't—" The press of the knife's tip to my lower lip cuts me off and I whine in protest.

He doesn't speak for a few moments. He just drags the tip

of the blade over my lips, pressing the point in against the bow of my upper lip until it stings. "What's my name?" he asks at last. "Not my real name, obviously. But the name I go by here. Do you know it?"

"Ravage." There's no hesitation when I say it. His is one of the few names I actually remember, and if I live through the night, I certainly won't forget.

"Good girl." Something unwanted curls up my spine at the purred praise, but I definitely don't need that tonight. "Do you remember anyone else's name?"

I think about it, going through the masks in my head before remembering another one. And the way the animal skull mask and the tactical gear were so similar to Ravage's. "Harrow."

"Oh, *very* good girl." He pauses, watching as I shift under him. "Do you like that, hmm? You like it when I call you my good girl?"

"Not at all." My fingers tighten again, and there's no way he doesn't feel it.

"Are you sure?" He leans down, his mask looming in my sight. "Are you—" I don't know why I do it. But when I get enough leverage with my feet pressed to the table and my fingers around his wrist, I lunge upward, cracking my forehead against the nose of his mask and making him reel back.

"Fuck!" he snarls, dropping the knife to the floor and lifting his hand to his face. "You little—" he snarls and his grip tightens, cutting off my air even as he laughs. "You're going to be fun, aren't you?"

"Let go!" I shriek, scratching at his wrist. "Let go, I can't—!"

"*Breathe?!*" he snarls near my face. "Of course you can't. Do you want to?" I nod fervently at his stupid question. "You think you deserve to breathe? Hmm? *Answer me.*" His snarl makes me flinch, and I nod again, desperate for some kind of relief from him choking me.

"Good girl." He releases my throat just enough for me to take a breath, his other hand coming up to grip my hoodie, tugging it up until my stomach is vulnerable to the cool air of the warehouse.

"Don't," I whisper, gripping his other wrist with one hand. "Don't!"

He just hums a reply, but doesn't stop until the fabric of my hoodie is bunched up under my bra. "Aren't you just so pretty?" His gloved hand strokes over my stomach, causing my muscles to tense up in desperate anticipation of the worst. "Especially all scared and breathless like this. Such a pretty Halloween present for me."

When I scoff a protest, his eyes flick back up to my face. "You're so lucky I enjoy it when you fight me. Some of the others wouldn't. I even like it when you cut me, and if I didn't think you'd kill me..." His fingers drift up my skin until he can trace the line of my bra. "I'd give you the knife back."

"I'll only stab you a little." The words are out of my mouth before I can stop them, and my pulse races with anxiety. "*Promise*."

His rough chuckle meets my ears. "I love that fight of yours, princess. I wonder how long you can keep it. I wonder what it'll take to have you begging for me, hmm?" He moves, shifting up on his knees, and his hand presses against my hip, dragging a whine of protest from me. But he ignores it as he drags my leggings over my hips, tugging them down my thighs even as I press my knees together in an attempt to stop him.

"No!" I fight Ravage again in earnest, one hand on the wrist at my throat and the other grasping for his other hand. "N-no! Don't! I don't want—" His fingers close lightly over the point in my neck that makes me see stars, and it clearly has the effect he's going for. My eyes close hard and with my focus on breathing around the pressure, Ravage is able to tug my leggings and underwear down to my knees amidst my choked off sob.

"I know, babe. You don't want any of this, do you?" I hate his mockingly sweet tone enough that I'd love to be the one choking him for a change. "You just came here looking for a fun haunt to push your boundaries, didn't you?" My heels hit the table again as I struggle, unable to look away from his mask as his gloved fingers trail over my hips before dipping between my thighs. "I'll push your boundaries for you." He says it like a promise, like a secret between us.

Before I can protest, or scream, or do anything, his fingers slide against me, his glove smooth against my folds. I yelp around his hand, both of mine flying up to claw at his wrist. But it only makes him shudder, and he tips his head back like he's getting off on the pain from my nails.

Maybe he is.

My whine echoes between us as he strokes his fingers against me, sliding against my entrance before pausing to give my clit extra attention. I hate it, or rather, I hate how my stomach curls in response to it and heat pools between my thighs at his urging. "Stop," I murmur, my nails digging in hard enough that I feel the slide of blood on his skin.

"Nah, princess. I'm having too much fun. Aren't you having fun?" he squeezes my throat again, cutting off my air, and his fingers pick up their movement against me, teasing my entrance between stroking over my clit every few seconds.

My head shakes in answer. I am most certainly not having fun. Especially not when he continues to not let me breathe until spots swim in my fuzzy vision. Only then does he let go, allowing me to gasp in a lungful of air just as he shoves two fingers into me.

"Feels good, right?" Ravage laughs. "With your head spinning and my fingers in your pretty pussy? You take two so easy. Bet you could take three." Again I shake my head in protest, writhing on the table to do anything to get away from him. "Deep breath, princess. On the count of three for me."

"N-no—please, I can't—"

"*One*," he growls, cutting me off as his fingers continue to thrust in and out of me languidly.

"I can't—"

"*Two*." I feel the brush of his third finger and whimper nervously, trying to press my thighs together while his hand continues to move as if he doesn't notice.

"Please—"

"Three. Deep breath."

I listen to him, though I don't want to. But I also don't want to suffocate while he fingers me. I suck in a deep breath and he waits until my lungs are full of oxygen before closing his fingers around my throat again, his thumb nudging that place under my jaw that makes me see stars. He's not kind about it. He doesn't slowly increase the pressure, but goes from just holding my neck to choking me so hard I can't even make a noise of protest.

"Good girl. *Good girl*," Ravage snarls, scissoring his fingers inside of me. "Look at you so desperate for me. Told you this would be better, didn't I? And you get so wet when I don't let you breathe. If I didn't have the gloves on, I bet you'd be able to hear just how much your pussy is begging for my fingers. So *fucking* greedy." Without warning, he adds another, sinking his digits into me slowly once before picking up his movements to be sharp and punishing. It jolts my hips against the table as I writhe, kicking out at nothing in a futile attempt to get him off of me while my lungs scream for oxygen.

"The more you fight, the faster you run out of oxygen." His

thumb finds my clit, rubbing over it continuously instead of just teasing like he'd done before. "Doesn't matter to me. I'm not the one who can't breathe. But I felt like I should tell you that."

I can barely hear him over the pounding of my pulse in my ears as my chest burns, begging for the oxygen he refuses to give me. My body shifts as his touches send heat jolting through me, and a soft whine is the only sound I can make in response.

"Feels so good, right?" Ravage purrs. "It's so intense when you can't breathe. Fuck, you're so wet. Will you come for me, princess?" He loosens his grip just a little, just enough for me to take a small breath before closing them around my throat again. "Are you?"

I shake my head fervently, fingers sliding against his bloody wrist. If I had the air I'd beg for him to stop. I'd *plead* with him to let me go, but all I can do is gasp around his hand and fight the rising heat from his touch.

He hums at my denial, twisting his fingers and curling them ever so slightly. The movement has me arching off the table, kicking out once again at nothing. "There you go. There it is, princess. You look like you feel so good. You wanna come for me?" Again I shake my head, mind starting to go fuzzy. When I open my eyes, darkness winks in and out of my vision, obscuring his mask as I try to blink enough to clear it.

I know there's nothing wrong with my eyes; it's the lack of oxygen that's doing this to me. When he brushes over my clit again, I let out a hoarse, gasping sob, chest heaving in a desperate attempt for oxygen.

"Come on, *come on*, my pretty little princess. You're so desperate, aren't you?" He leans in close until he can nuzzle his mask against the side of my face. "It'll feel so good, I promise.

Just let go for me. Just let go and come all over my fingers, pretty girl."

This time I can't even shake my head. My vision is darkening, his mask is mostly shadows in my unfocused gaze, and my body feels coiled and tense, the actions of his fingers only making it worse. My hips jerk against his hand, and I can't seem to help myself as I continue to grind against his fingers, even when I distantly hear his soft murmurs of encouragement.

"You won't last much longer. Come on, Noa." His grip changes, softening very slightly and making my head spin. "Come for me, babe. Come on my fingers. Soak my glove in your cum, princess." He seems to be working himself up as well, as his fingers thrust desperately in and out of my body until finally, I can't help it. Eyes wide and mostly unseeing, I arch off the table, my grip loosening on his wrist as my orgasm hits me.

And that's when he lets go.

Oxygen floods my lungs as I come, loud cries leaving my mouth like sobs as I audibly drag air into my lungs. Ravage fingers me through it, not even slowing down while my body tenses around him.

"Stop," I pant weakly, the feeling overwhelming as I come down from my release. "S-stop. It's too much, it's too—" He instantly does what I ask, sitting back on his heels as he watches me from behind the mask.

"Good girl. You're such a good girl for me, aren't you?" He reaches up and smears his gloved fingers over my lips, forcing them between my teeth so I'm forced to taste my release on his gloves. It turns my stomach, and I really should be more grossed out.

I shouldn't be aching from the best orgasm I've ever had in my life. It's clearly the oxygen deprivation talking as he strokes his fingers over my tongue, wordlessly watching me. "Good girl," he murmurs again. "Just lay there and breathe for me. I'll give you a minute."

Opening my eyes, I turn away from him, trying to pant out the question of what he means. But he jerks my face back up to face him, keeping his gaze on mine. "But just a minute, okay? I don't know how much longer I can wait to feel your sweet pussy around my cock."

6

With my head spinning and finally able to breathe without his hand on my throat, I stare up at Ravage with narrowed eyes. My hands fall to the table, gripping the edges of it as I shudder under him. His now-free hand goes to my stomach, fingers splaying against my pale skin.

"Poor little princess," he coos. "One would think you've never been fucked within an inch of your life before. You act like you might not be looking forward to it."

"I hate you." The words are soft on my tongue, and I flinch when he lifts his other hand, only to pluck at his glove until the hand I'd cut is bare.

He hums in response, flexing his fingers as he studies the shallow cut that's smeared blood across his skin. "I can tell. You've cut me twice, and I like to think I'm pretty quick on the uptake, pretty girl. I think I can change your mind, though." He drops both hands to trail them up my thighs, causing me to shudder against the table. "At least let me *try* to get you to like me." His words are soft and promising, and he shifts on my thighs to lean over me on his knees, hands braced on either side of my head. "Promise I'll make you feel so good. Promise you'll enjoy everything...even if it hurts." He leans down, bending on his elbows like he's going to kiss me. Instead, he nuzzles at my throat, his soft murmurs of approval barely audible over my harsh breaths.

I wonder if he's realized that he's given me a bit more wiggle room. I stay still, not wanting him to notice, and tilt my head back as if I'm giving him better access to my neck.

Remembering the knife, I run the memory through my head, making sure I know where he dropped it. I can't turn my head to check, but I'm relatively sure that it's on the floor to my left. Taking a breath, I count myself down silently, terrified that this is going to go extremely poorly.

I have a bad feeling if I fuck this up, I won't get another chance for a while. *Or ever.* I suck in another breath, just as he lifts his head, and bring my knees up under him to kick upward as hard as I can, nailing him in the stomach.

He yelps in surprise and pain, reeling backward, and another kick sends him crashing to the floor behind the table. I scramble off the table as well, hitting the ground on my knees hard as I drag my leggings back up over my hips. The knife glitters in the light from a window as I lunge for it, Ravage's yells of fury spurring me forward.

Somehow, I manage to grab it and stumble to my feet, whirling on him just as he lunges in my direction. The blade between us stops him short, however, and he jerks to a stop a few inches from the tip of the blade that I hold in one shaking hand.

"I can't decide if I'm more irritated at being kicked in the stomach or turned on by how fucking feral you are, princess," Ravage snorts, moving to prowl around me but not coming any closer.

"I'd be way too irritated by the kick to think about

anything else," I snap, never lowering the knife as I turn to keep him in front of me. "But that's just me."

"We can fix that. Just takes practice to learn to get through the pain." He lifts his shirt with his gloved hand, revealing a very toned abdomen and muscles that clearly have a very intimate relationship with the gym. Or rather, some form of workout. He presses his bare fingers just over his right hip as I watch, pressing down slightly with a groan. "You sure did get me good." He laughs ruefully. "But now I have to worry about you hurting me with that knife again."

"You're only worried I'll end your fun early," I snap, sneering at him in frustration and panic. "You're going to kill me anyway, so don't act so magnanimous and full of concern."

"Such a big word for a terrified little girl." Ravage drops his shirt and holds his hands up, as if in surrender. But I don't believe him for a second. "And yeah, you caught me. I'll probably kill you when I'm done. I would prefer not to spend the rest of my life in jail, thanks very much."

Rolling my eyes, I shift my grip on the knife to hold it more firmly in my clammy fingers. "Pretty sure I said I'd keep my mouth shut if you let me go. Remember?"

His snort nearly cuts me off, and I can almost *feel* his disbelief. "Oh, please. Don't lie to me or yourself. You were never going to stay quiet. Not without either a little help, a lot of convincing, or…" He rolls his shoulders in a shrug. "Like I said. I wouldn't look cute in prison-chic orange."

He lunges forward suddenly, giving me almost no warning as his hands reach for me. But I've been expecting something, I drop to one knee, ignoring the pain from hitting the concrete floor as I duck under his reach. This time I shove him in the back, using his momentum so he keeps going straight into a pile of wood and metal on the floor. He lands with a crash that I'm sure my long dead grandmother can hear from beyond the grave, but I don't stick around to see if I somehow, luckily, killed him.

I doubt any part of my night is going to go that smoothly.

He groans in the heap, proving me right, and I take off at a run across the room, finding another door and hitting it hard to shove it open. He'd said the only way out was through the lobby, but nothing in me believes him. Why wouldn't he lie to me, after all, just so I don't try for another escape from the warehouse?

Distantly I worry about running into one of the others, but that's a problem for future me. Right now I focus on the new hallway I'm in, wondering why the hell there are so many fucking *hallways* in a warehouse.

Voices from the end of the hall send a bolt of panic through me, and I look around the space, finding a door close to me and praying it's open. The knob turns in my grip, revealing a small storage closet that definitely isn't my first choice, but I'll take what I can get.

I step inside and close the door, backing up to the shelves on the wall. I feel objects shift behind me, and I move to get more comfortable with a quick, silent prayer that I don't knock anything to the floor.

A door opens and closes, and a girl's voice echoes along the walls of the hallway. Two people pass in front of my door, judging by their shadows that block out the light under the door for a second or two each. But they don't stop. They don't even slow down at my door.

It feels like they aren't even looking for me.

"It gets easier," a girl murmurs. "You'll be okay. Next year you'll be able to focus on…" Another door opens and closes, cutting off their conversation before I even know what it's about.

But I wait until I'm sure there's no one in the hallway, or as reasonably sure as I can be. Finally I reach out, moving toward the door, only to feel a tug on my hoodie that makes me choke on the breath I'd taken. I can barely turn to see, and when I do, I find I'm caught on a hook hanging from the shelf I'd backed up into. More than one, judging by just how tightly I'm stuck. I tug, saying a prayer for my soon to be ripped hoodie, and promise myself to find another one just like it after tonight. It's not like I'll ever be able to get the blood out of this one, anyway.

But it doesn't rip. It doesn't come free, either, no matter how hard I tug or how I move it. "What the fuck?" I hiss, yanking on it until I hear the slight tearing of fabric. Still, I don't feel any slack. Not yet. I tug again, but I can't get the fabric to tear, and I'm starting to wonder if I'm going to have to leave it here.

God, I really, *really* don't want to try to escape this place in just my skull-patterned bra and leggings. That feels like a snuff film waiting to happen. On the other hand, twisting around isn't doing it, and finally I decide I'll have to wiggle out of it and unhook it when it's off.

Or rip it, depending on how bad it is.

I'm just about to pull my arm free of my sleeve when a door creaks open again, making me freeze in place. I'm too afraid to make any noise, and I hold my breath to wait for whoever it is to leave the hallway so I can get myself free. Their footsteps get closer, and a shadow passes under the door, but they stop for a moment, blocking the light from the door.

Seconds tick by until finally their shadow disappears and their steps retreat again, quickly becoming inaudible.

"Thank God," I mutter, sucking in a breath to calm my pulse. Once again, I reach for my sleeve, my fingers curled around the hem of it just as the door opens wide, light spilling into the dark closet.

Harrow stands there, studying me from behind the animal mask while I just stare back. His head tilts to the side, and he turns to glance down the hallway while my brain reboots from the shock of him just *knowing* I was here. Before I can even begin to come up with a plan, he steps into the room, snatches the knife off of the shelf I'd set it on, and closes the door behind him to plunge us into darkness once again.

7

The first thought to go through my mind is that he has the knife.

The second is that I'm absolutely screwed and still stuck to the shelf behind me. I stand in place, frozen, the closet barely big enough for both of us. Even with me pressed back against the shelves as hard as I can be, I can still feel the heat radiating from his body only centimeters in front of me.

But I can't say anything. I can't seem to find the words, and I worry that if I'm the first to break the silence in this small, dark place, somehow this will be real. Somehow, it'll be *worse*.

A touch on my cheek makes me flinch, and a low whine bubbles from my lips as leather-gloved fingers stroke my along my jaw. When I start moving, trying to writhe against him, I hear a soft murmur from behind the mask, though it's barely there and almost inaudible.

"W-what?" I gasp, head jerking up to search the darkness for his mask. But it really is so dark in here, and all I can see from the light under the door is a vague silhouette.

But he doesn't speak again, nor bother to repeat himself as

he leans in close. I hear the shift of something above me, and I can feel the brush of his arm against my hair as he settles forward to lean against the shelves behind me. Which, of course, presses the length of his body to mine, an unyielding wall between me and escape.

"Stop," I whisper, jerking on my hoodie to try to free myself. "*Stop,*" I say again, stronger this time, and shove against his chest.

Harrow only chuckles. It's a low, soft sound from behind his mask, and he leans forward until the plastic of his mask brushes my cheek. "But I haven't even done anything to you yet," he murmurs in my ear; the words are so soft it feels like he's telling me some kind of clandestine secret. His voice is deeper than Ravage's, though I can't tell much else about it. His hand on my jaw moves, blindly pushing my hair back behind my ear softly, gently.

Like he fucking *cares.*

My soft growl of protest only makes him huff a soft chuckle. Without warning, he presses his palm over my mouth, gripping both sides of my jaw and pushing my head back against the shelf behind me. Again I feel the brush of his mask against my face, and I close my eyes at the fearful anticipation that has my stomach twisting with panic and...something I refuse to name.

"I'm not like Rav," he murmurs. "I don't get off on you fighting me and making me hurt. In fact"—his fingers flex in warning, tightening painfully on my jaw—"I suggest you do what I say, little girl. I won't hesitate to *discipline* you if you need to be convinced to behave."

Fuck. A shudder goes through me that's not quite from fear, and I whine behind his hand as he pulls back. Again, I jerk against the shelf, ready to wiggle out of my hoodie if that's what it'll take to get free. Even though I'm fully aware that my hoodie being stuck is no longer my biggest problem.

Harrow is.

His fingers slide down my jaw, stroking over my neck and causing me to shudder with the memory of how it felt to come with Ravage's grip so tight I couldn't breathe. That makes him chuckle, as if he *knows* what I'm thinking, but his hand doesn't stop. Instead, it disappears, and he leans against me as his hands stroke up my back, dragging my hoodie up with him.

For some reason, I'm more terrified of him than I was of Ravage. He's just so quiet, and not nearly so playful. This feels more *serious*, somehow. Even though this whole damn thing is the epitome of serious and terrifying.

"N-no," I breathe as his hands move to my front to continue pushing my hoodie up and up. I grip his wrists blindly in the dark, gazing up at where I think his eyes might be behind his mask. "Don't—" He grabs my sides in a bruising grip, pulling a yelp from my throat, which has him huffing a soft sound of amusement.

When I say nothing else, his grip loosens. All I can bring myself to do is writhe as he drags my hoodie up further, easily tugging it over my head and arms until I'm left in my bra and leggings in the cold closet. Shivering, I flinch when I feel his hands back on my body. He cups my jaw in one hand while the gloved fingers of the other skim the bottom of my bra, tracing the line of it under my breasts.

Trembling, I reach up to grip his wrist at my jaw, somehow less afraid to touch this hand than the other one. "Wait." The word is out of my mouth before I can help it. "Please, I just—" One handed, he unhooks the clasp of my bra nestled between my cleavage, causing the material to fall to either side before he smoothly pushes it off of my arms to fall to the floor.

The moment I move to cover myself, he shifts to grip my

wrists in one hand and pushes them up above my head. The hold is so tight, it feels like my bones are grinding together in his grip as my hands press almost painfully against the shelves.

He doesn't seem to mind that it's dark. The fact doesn't deter him from cupping my breasts in his hand, the slide of leather smooth against my skin. My back arches instinctively, a whine escaping from my lips when his thumb brushes over my nipple.

"I don't—" His fingers tighten around my wrist, and his hand moves to knead my breast almost painfully. The warning is clear, and I close my eyes hard in the darkness, as if that will change any of this somehow.

He takes his fucking time teasing me. Exploring my bare upper body with his fingers and his palm until I'm quite literally shaking against the shelves, tremors going through my body no matter how much I try to keep myself still. My breathing is the only sound in the darkness of the closet, and I'm glad he can't see my face.

I'm not sure I'm keeping it together well, and that probably shows very clearly in my expression. At least in the dark I can deny it, and he can't see how—

My gasp of surprise is loud in the small space as Harrow shoves me to my knees, his hands on my shoulders to keep me there. Instinctively, I reach up, one hand pressed to his thigh and the other on his wrist like I'm going to dig my nails into his skin. But the moment I even brush my nails against him, he lets out a long, low sigh that is very clear.

Especially when his grip on my shoulder tightens to the point of pain. It's enough to make me let him go, and I drop my hand like his skin is scalding.

His hands leave my shoulders, but I'm not exactly left confused about what he's doing. Not when I hear the clink of his belt buckle and the sound of a zipper being pulled down. My stomach twists with dread and I jerk back, as if I can go anywhere at all when I'm basically straddling his boots on my sore knees. The floor under me is hard and unforgiving, and the cold from the concrete is stealing the warmth of my skin, making me shudder.

I flinch when his fingers smooth over my hair, stroking my head like I'm his favorite pet. He's so relaxed and unhurried in his motions, which somehow makes this worse. At least with Ravage, I had some idea of what he was doing, and tried to use his impatience to my advantage.

It had gone pretty well, if I do say so myself.

But Harrow is *different*. He's terrifying in a different way, and I'm so fucking scared of him that I can't even bring myself to consider hurting him in the ways I'd hurt Ravage.

His fingers twining through my hair pulls me back to the present. Instead of petting me again, he grips my hair, not quite hard enough to hurt as long as I don't try to yank away. "Please…" I murmur, part of me wishing I could see his face in the dark. At least his eyes behind the mask, but all I can really see from the scant light from the hallway are the outlines of his boots and legs.

Harrow doesn't acknowledge my pleas. He guides my face closer to him until I feel the tip of his cock slide against my lower lip. I inhale sharply, jerking in his grip, but he holds me completely still with just his hand in my hair, fingers tightening in warning.

At his urging, I open my mouth, lips parted, but he continues to tease me. He presses himself between my lips, just enough for me to feel him on my tongue, before pulling out and letting his cock rest against my lip. My breaths come in anticipatory huffs from my open mouth, and he shudders at the feeling, though his grip doesn't waver in my hair. He doesn't pull back whatsoever, and instead slowly thrusts into my mouth once more, until I have to relax my jaw in order to keep my teeth off of him.

I'm pretty sure that would get me in a world of trouble, even without him saying so. He pulls back again, his movements slow and steady and a little teasing. All I can do is wait until he presses back in, deeper this time.

My hand comes up, my fingers hooking over his belt with a soft sound of protest. He doesn't do anything to retaliate. He doesn't even seem to mind, so I grip his belt more confidently, a whine building between my lips as he continues to push deeper.

God, he's fucking *big*. My protesting whine is loud in the darkness as he keeps going, his fingers in my hair are still tight enough I can't go anywhere or do anything except take it. "Relax," I hear him murmur when he feels my jolt from his cock brushing the back of my tongue. "Just relax, little girl." His words are comforting murmurs, but they do nothing to stop the trembling in my thighs or the way I grasp desperately to his belt.

Finally, after what feels like eternity, my nose presses to his skin, his entire length between my lips as he just holds me there like he enjoys the feeling of this. Just this, without anything else.

And with his soft exhale, maybe he does. Instinctively, I try to swallow, but the action just makes me jerk in discomfort while I try not to choke.

"Better not," he warns. But he doesn't follow it up with anything as he holds me there, his cock heavy and warm between my lips and on my tongue.

Finally he pulls his hips back a little, only to press them forward quickly, burying himself in my throat again amidst my sounds of protest. He does it again, and again; each movement is faster and a little more forceful than the last until he's fucking my mouth with thrusts that have me shuddering.

My eyes water from the strain, and whines of discomfort sound around his cock whenever I have the breath for it. My throat already burns from Ravage choking me, and this certainly isn't doing me any favors.

I can't even swallow, so with a groan of frustration, I swipe away the saliva trickling down my chin with my free hand I can't seem to decide what to do with. *God,* I wish I had the nerve to bite him. But I don't even have the guts to hit him or sink my nails into his skin. There's no way I can do something arguably worse.

Not to mention he's so hard to read. He does nothing except fuck my mouth at his leisure, seeming unhurried and unbothered by anything else. Surely he has to consider that I could bite him, that I could absolutely sink my teeth into his cock and make this a *really* bad night for him as well.

It seems stupid to trust me when I'm definitely here against my will.

He pulls himself free, using his tip to trace my lower lip again as his grip softens in my hair. "Take a deep breath for me, sweetheart," he tells me almost kindly as I swallow around the burn in my throat.

"Wait—" His grip tightens again, making me squirm on my knees and shiver in the cold closet. It's as much of a warning as I need, so I fall silent and pant in shaky, nervous breaths. He gives me a few seconds before repeating himself.

"Deep breath." He strokes over my hair as he says it, before readjusting his grip so his glove scrapes against my scalp. I'm too afraid to not do what he says. So, I take a deep breath and he thrusts into my mouth, burying himself all the way until I choke, tears streaming down my face from my watering eyes.

But he doesn't let go or pull away this time. He holds me

against him, my nose pressed to his skin as I writhe and try not to panic.

"Breathe through your nose." He still sounds so patient, so unworried. I can't stand how casual he seems, even when I'm having a fit with my mouth on his cock.

I do what he says without him needing to repeat it, trembling as I kneel on the dirty floor of a warehouse closet with a masked man's cock buried in my throat. The thought makes a nervous sound bubble up my throat, and I can't help but think of how ridiculous this would sound if I were ever to tell anyone.

But first, I have to make it out of here alive.

He moves again, but not so nicely this time. He fucks my face with deliberate, measured strokes, his length sliding against my tongue over and over. I swear I hear his purred praises, soft behind his mask, but my ears are full of the rush of blood and lack of oxygen while I keep my mouth open wide enough for my jaw to ache.

It isn't until his rhythm falters that I realize he's close to coming. The thought has me jerking backward, but the sound of his quiet, cruel laugh is stark in the closet. "No, little girl. You're going to swallow it like a good girl." His fingers tighten in my hair, a blatant threat, and I close my eyes desperately, a whine of protest in my throat.

Harrow doesn't seem to give a damn. He doesn't care one bit as he continues to use my mouth how he wants. His movements become faster, more erratic, and my grip on his belt tightens in response until he slams into me one final time. Once again, I find my nose pressed to his skin, but this time he holds me there as his cock pulses against my tongue with his release.

He doesn't say anything. Doesn't speak or make a sound as he comes with his hand in my hair and his length so far down my throat I have no real choice *but* to swallow. With a sigh, he pulls back, hand still in my hair, and gives my hair a quick, warning squeeze before he shifts backward to tuck himself into his black cargo pants. I can hear the sound of his zipper and the clink of his belt again, while my head spins and I focus more on breathing and calming myself down. The feel and taste of him is still heady on my tongue, and I wipe my wrist across my mouth with a frown I'm glad he can't see.

His hands are back a few seconds later, cradling my face between them sweetly. "What am I going to do with you?" he murmurs with a heavy sigh that sends a flicker of dread up my spine. "My sweet, stupid little girl."

8

Whatever I'm going to say, or do, or cry for is cut off by the sound of a gunshot. Harrow stiffens, one hand coming down to rest against my hair like he's trying to comfort or reassure me. He sighs, low and long, and a second later my hoodie is dropped onto my head from the shelf above. I flinch but only take a moment before pulling it on over my head, not caring that I don't have my bra as I scramble to my feet.

"If you know what's good for you..." Harrow pins me back against the shelves, fingers stroking along my jaw. "You'll stay right here while I figure out—" Another gunshot goes off, causing me to jump in surprise. He sighs once more, seeming more irritated than anything, and turns to open the door to the hallway.

"Stay," he orders, as the light from the hallway illuminates the animal skull mask obscuring his face. Then he closes the closet door, leaving me alone in the dark once again, but this time with no weapon.

But I am for sure not going to *stay put*. When I hear another door open, I give it a few more seconds before creeping out into the hallway, wishing I still had the knife I stabbed Ravage with. But either way, I can't just huddle in the closet. I can't just hide and wait for him to come back, since I'm pretty sure Harrow is ready to slit my throat and throw me into a pit with the other dead bodies in the warehouse.

That thought makes me remember the eye squishing between my fingers, and I almost wretch. A shudder goes through me as I jog down the hallway silently toward the cracked open door leading to a different side of the warehouse. I hesitate, wondering if I should go back to the open area I know leads to the lobby and try to figure out a way to leave from there, since I know for a fact there's a door to take me outside.

But I already tried that route, and it hadn't worked out for me.

"Fuck it," I murmur, biting down on my lower lip before slowly opening the door further with my fingertips. It leads me into another big room, though this one is lined with larger glass windows I could probably jump through if I'm brave enough to tough out all the glass shards raking through my skin. I look around, surprised that it's actually sort of well lit, and my eyes land on tables spaced along the wall, each of them covered with stacks and piles of different things.

And different *masks*. A few of the masks I recognize are there. The doll mask, the clown mask, and the scarecrow hood. But the emperor mask isn't, and neither is the distorted ghost mask. There are normal clothes on some of the tables, jeans and t-shirts, while a black lacy dress is draped over the table that's littered with maimed toys and a doll mask.

I step closer, reaching out to run my fingers over the doll-like mask before moving on to the next table. The room is large enough that I don't immediately hear the murmur of voices until a hysterical, snarling laugh rings against the glass above me. Being this close to the windows, I realize my plan of jumping through them was a little too ambitious when I'd have to *climb* up to them in the first place.

Unfortunately, there are no weapons on the tables. Just props and costumes and a few scattered papers. But I walk down the line until I get to the end, where there's a pile of normal clothes, a set of keys, and a wallet thrown haphazardly onto the table. I've only just opened it to see messy auburn hair on the ID peeking out of a pocket when another gunshot rings out, causing me to drop the wallet with a wince.

Voices echo through the room, bouncing off the walls enough that I can't hear what's being said. I know I should find somewhere to hide or look for a phone, at the very least. But instead I find myself creeping toward the other side of the room that's blocked by a large concrete wall passing through the middle of the space like a large divider.

I hug the concrete, pressed up against it, with my eyes wide and fixed on where I think the voices are coming from. Sure enough, when I'm mostly around it, I see both Harrow and Ravage circling a man I recognize from the lobby, though with a few less fingers now, covered in blood, and holding a gun. When he looks up at me, I realize he's also missing a fucking *eye.*

My stomach turns over at the sight, and I have to look down at the floor to swallow rapidly in order to prevent myself from puking.

"I-I recognize you." The man's desperate, rough voice croaks out of his throat, but I don't look up at him. "You were in the lobby, you—" He takes a breath to steady himself, and when I glance at him I see him point the gun at Harrow and Ravage in succession.

"You need to call the police," he tells me. "There has to be a phone around here. We have to get out of here...we have to see who's still alive, and—"

"There's no one still alive other than you, dumbass." Ravage cackles, prowling around a table and tapping his fingers on it rhythmically. "And Noa can't help you. Why the hell would she put herself at risk for something like *you*?" He sneers the word like an insult, making my stomach twist.

When the man looks at me, I have to look away, unable to meet his eyes. I hate to say it, but Ravage is right. As much as I might want to help this man, he's a stranger, and I don't want to get murdered by the two men in masks, or anyone else still prowling around the warehouse.

"Sorry," I murmur, eyeing him regretfully. I step back, creating a bit more distance between us, and I hear the anguished snarl that leaves him at my action.

"You're picking *them*? After what they did? *Look at what they did to me, you stupid bitch*!" The insult isn't what I'm expecting, but I drag my gaze up to his face, taking in his gory eye socket and the stumps of three of his fingers on one hand. The other hand isn't looking so great either, truthfully. His skin seems to have been peeled back, like a butcher peeling the skin off of a dead cow to reveal the meat underneath.

But that comparison does absolutely nothing for my stomach or the way my throat clenches shut in an attempt to stall the nausea clawing its way up my esophagus.

"I'm sorry," I whisper. "I'm so—" My heart stutters to a halt in my chest when the man points the gun at me with shaking, unsteady fingers.

"Then you can die with them," he sneers, shifting his grip on the weapon.

Everything seems to move in slow motion. I stand there, frozen. But from the corner of my eye, I see Ravage lunge forward, covering the distance between them and reaching out to grab the man's arm. He yanks it upward just as the gun goes off, and distantly I hear the shattering of a skylight while my eyes are fixed on the scene in front of me.

Ravage slams the man's hand down onto a nearby table, sending the gun spinning out of his grip. Harrow is there a moment later, forcing the man back down after he wrenches himself up.

"Ah, ah, ah." Harrow's purr is soft. "Hex may have had first dibs on you, but"—he leans down, gloved fingers trailing across the man's face—"she's not here anymore, so you're fair game for any of us."

My gaze slides down away from them, even amidst the man's screams as Harrow does something to his face I know I don't want to see. I hear wet, thick sounds that make my stomach turn, and I force myself not to look back up, no matter how curious I am.

I have a feeling I won't be able to deal with what I see. Instead, my eyes gravitate toward the gun on the floor between me and the men, and my heart races as I consider it.

Neither Harrow nor Ravage seem to notice. Not even when I take one careful step away from the wall.

Then another.

One more takes me in range of it, and I kneel down to reach out with one trembling hand, fingers closing around the still-warm and bloody metal before I jerk back to my feet.

"*Noa.*" Harrow's voice is disapproving, though he sounds more like a disappointed parent than someone worried about getting shot by their victim-to-be. I glance up at him, biting down on my lower lip, and step back until my back hits the concrete wall again. He lifts a hand and crooks two gloved fingers at me once, then again, beckoning for me to give him the gun.

"You're joking," I breathe, watching as Ravage lets the

man's mangled body slither to the floor in a heap. I can't look at him. Especially not when I can see the fresh blood and gore staining his face that I *refuse* to focus on.

Besides, that man is very dead now, so he's no longer a concern of mine. I can't let him be, if I want to have any hope of getting out of here with my life intact.

"You...you think I'll give you the gun because you wiggled your fingers at me?" A shiver goes through me, and I lean my head back against the wall. My knees want to buckle, and every part of me just wants to run to my bed, throw the covers over myself, and hide for the next thirty years or so. But the ridiculousness of his request makes me giggle, the muffled sound escaping my clenched teeth.

Harrow just huffs out a breath, but it's Ravage who prowls closer to me, vibrating with excitement.

"I'll do more than wiggle my fingers at you, princess," he purrs, barely pausing when I lift the gun to point it directly at his chest. "Want me to come get it from you? Shall I peel your fingers off of it one by one while you cry and beg me to stop? Tell you what..." He holds up his hands, peeling off his gloves before reaching out to me with his fingers twitching expectantly. "You give me that gun right now"—he takes a step toward me—"and I'll make sure Harrow is gentle with you. Sort of. I'll even rein myself in a little when I fuck your pretty pussy."

"And if I say I'd rather keep it so I can shoot you if the mood takes me?" My voice is rough from exhaustion and being choked out, but I never look away from him as he prowls closer to me.

"Then I'll have to take it from you, princess. And then Harrow is going to be so *mean* to you." He glances back at the animal skull masked man behind him, who stands completely at ease with his arms crossed loosely over his chest. His head tilts to the side, and even though I can't see his eyes, I can feel the weight of his gaze on me. "And I'll remember that you need a lesson in following directions. You don't want that."

I shift my weight from foot to foot. "I really don't want that," I agree, a tremor going up my spine. "All I want is to go home."

"Oh, yeah?" With his hand still held out, Ravage moves toward me until the gun is pressed between his collarbones, at the hollow of his throat. "You want to tell me all about it, princess? You want to—"

He stops talking when I pull the trigger reflexively, without even having to think about it. But when the gun clicks around an empty chamber, the two of us just stand there, and my face falls as I realize something very important.

The gun is empty.

I pull the trigger again, then once more for good measure, before Ravage lunges forward to knock the gun from my hand, sending it spinning across the floor. I dart to the side, or try to, but Ravage slams me into the wall, fingers going around my throat easily and quickly. This time, though, it's the warm press of his palm against my throat, instead of the slide of his gloves.

"Oh, *Noa*." He *tsks* at me, shaking his head slowly from side to side. "That was the wrong choice, princess. But that's okay. I'm not mad at you." He curls closer to me, his body pressed to mine. "I'll just have to teach you how to make better choices, won't I?"

9

Before I can think of what to say or do or *scream*, Harrow strides closer, reaching out to tilt my chin up to him, eyes studying mine from behind the mask. "Let me," he murmurs, reaching out and grabbing Ravage by the back of the throat. When the other man growls his protest, Harrow turns on him, lifting his chin in a taunting challenge. "Rav..." he warns, grip tightening. "Do *you* want a lesson on how to behave? In front of Noa, no less?"

That definitely shouldn't make my stomach twist in anticipation, and I drop my gaze to the floor, glaring at the gun that's a few yards away. If it had been loaded, I wouldn't be in this mess right now. Probably. Though, I'd also be a murderer, which doesn't sound so great either.

But the thought makes me giggle, and I press a hand over my mouth even as the two of them look at me. "Sorry, I'm sorry," I ramble, closing my eyes.

"What's so funny, princess?" Ravage relaxes into Harrow's hold, leaning up to nuzzle his mask against the taller man's throat in a show of submission before Harrow lets go of him.

"No, it's just..." I shrug my shoulders. "Here I am, debating what's worse. The gun being not loaded, so now I'm probably going to get murdered by two men in Halloween masks at *the wrong fucking extreme haunt*. Or the gun being loaded, making me a fucking murderer for shooting you in the throat." Closing my eyes hard, I drop my hand to press them both against the wall behind me before lifting my face and opening my eyes to look between them. "And I can't decide which would be worse."

They trade a look and Ravage scoffs softly under his breath, reaching out to tuck my hair that's completely come undone from the ponytail it had been in behind my ear. "I was never in any danger," he purrs. "If I hadn't known the gun was empty, I wouldn't have let you press it to my throat."

I shake my head, grinning humorlessly. "That's probably not the comfort you think it is." Sucking in a breath, I press back against the wall behind me, the concrete cool against my palms. "Let me go. Please," I say, keeping my voice level and no note of pleading or begging anywhere to be found. "I really, literally won't tell anyone. What would I even say? 'Some crazy people in masks killed people in a warehouse that I don't know the address of, officer'?" I tilt my head to the side, glaring at them incredulously. "Come on. Who's going to believe that?"

The two of them trade a look before Ravage sighs and shakes his head. "I expected begging," he admits. "I'm pretty thrilled you *aren't* begging for us not to kill you, admittedly. That gets really boring, really fast. But..."—he tips his head to the side, studying me from behind the skeleton mask—"we still have a lesson to teach you about making good choices, remember?" He casts a look at Harrow just as I glance to the side, debating whether I could make it to the nearest door.

"We'll take her to your room. I guess it was worth you dragging that stupid mattress in there after all." Harrow cuffs

Ravage lightly on the shoulder, making the other man sneer a laugh.

When he turns to me, I bolt, but I only make it two steps before I'm hauled off my feet and thrown over Ravage's shoulder, my breath leaving me in a gasp. "Put me down!" I protest, kicking against his chest. My hand comes up, slipping against his shoulder, as I try to get some kind of leverage to kick him again.

At least, until he pins my legs against his chest. "So *feisty*, princess," he laughs. "I love it. But I don't need my chest all bruised up, so you're gonna have to wait until we get there." He strides purposefully toward one side of the room, his foot connecting with the door hard enough to make me wince and causing it to slam open on its hinges.

Harrow follows him, casual and unbothered, just shaking his head at the now-dented door before he closes it behind him and trails us down a hallway. I glare up at the animal mask, meeting his thoughtful gaze before dropping my eyes back down to the floor and the occasional glimpse of Harrow's boots.

Another door is shoved open in front of Ravage, and suddenly I'm no longer on his shoulder. My feet hit the floor hard, and the man catches me, holding onto my arms until I regain my balance. Not that I plan on thanking him.

Why the hell would I?

Instead, I look at the door, making one last desperate move for it just as Harrow closes it behind him, and a hand comes up to twist in the front of my hoodie. "There you go again, making bad choices," he sighs softly with a tinge of disappointment in his tone. He walks forward without letting go of me, backing me up across the space until I'm in the middle of the windowless, starkly lit room. I glance around, looking for anything to help me, only seeing a large armchair that's definitely seen better days, and a mattress covered in mismatched blankets in the corner.

"How prison chic," I mutter, glaring at Ravage. "It's very you."

He snorts and collapses into the armchair to face us, one leg folding over the other. "I'd watch what you say if I were you, princess. Harrow is a lot less playful and...*forgiving* than me. If you'd cut him with that knife and kicked him off that table, well..." He rolls his shoulders in a shrug. "He might not have seen it for the fun game it was."

Frankly, I hadn't seen it as such a *fun game* either. But I figure now isn't the time to press that point. Especially when Harrow jerks me forward, lifting me onto my toes by my hoodie. "Get on your knees." His voice is soft. Casual. Like he's asked me to pass a box of pasta.

"What?"

He doesn't repeat himself, but his dark eyes narrow behind his mask. He sighs, switching his grip to yank me harder onto my toes, still not repeating himself before he finally lets go. His eyes flash in a silent, pointed warning, and I find myself slowly getting to my knees, hoping not to bruise them any more than they already are.

I can't help the rush of anxiety that goes through me as he just fucking *stares* at me from behind the mask, eyes narrowed shrewdly. But I do sit back on my heels, figuring I have nothing better to do. At least, until his voice makes me tense up all over again.

"Did you notice, Rav...?" His voice is soft. Casual. Almost affectionate as Harrow taps the toe of his boot on the floor. "Back in the lobby, when our little unexpected visitor was supposed to be watching the video, she wasn't paying attention. She couldn't keep her eyes off of my boots...could you, little girl?"

When I don't answer, he reaches out to grip my chin and forces me to look up at him. "I asked you a question."

"I..." This is definitely not what I'd expected him to say. "Y-yeah, I guess. Your boots are pretty cool."

"I think you like them a bit more than that. I was waiting for you to start drooling over them. So you can do that now." He releases me, staring at me expectantly, but I just...look at him.

"You want me to what?" I ask, stunned and not sure my brain is working right.

"I want you to show me just how much you like my boots. Do you need some help with that?" When I don't answer or move, seeing as I'm too stunned and *way* too confused about what he means, he reaches out to tangle his fingers in my hair. He gives me a second, then two, before suddenly he drags me down to the floor, shoving my face to his boot and holding me there. "Show me how much you like my boots, pretty girl," Harrow purrs. "I think my meaning is pretty clear at this point, and you're not stupid."

I'm not. But this isn't something I've ever considered being into, and it feels more than a little embarrassing. I feel like a fucking *dog* being shoved to the floor for doing something bad, and I can't help but writhe, my fingers pressing to the concrete floor as I start to push up against his hand again.

But he doesn't let me. He shoves me back down until my nose is pressed to the smooth leather of his boot, hard enough to sting. "Okay!" I gasp. "I won't try to get up—"

"And I'll let go once you know what to do." His words cut me off smoothly, and he holds me in place, stuck to them. *Fuck*, this is humiliating. I can't stop thinking about how Ravage is only a few feet away, watching me squirm on the floor with my face against Harrow's boot.

I'm also not being given much of a choice about it,

however. With a soft sound of protest I open my mouth, licking over the smooth surface of his boot with a shudder at the taste of dirty leather. I can't let myself think about what he's stood in, or how much blood he's gotten on these. I can only focus on licking over the toe of his boot and hoping he'll decide it's good enough in the next few seconds.

"Don't sit up. Not until I tell you that you're done," Harrow warns. He uncurls his fingers from my hair and stands up straight, hands in his pockets as he stares down at me. I'm too terrified of him to do anything other than what he tells me. So I continue to run my tongue over the leather with a shudder, one hand inching up to grip the back of his ankle as I lean forward to lap at the leather surrounding his ankle as well.

I *swear* I hear a soft murmur of approval from the man above me, but it's hard to tell over Rav's delighted groan from the armchair. "Now I wish I'd worn boots like yours," he chuckles. "*Fuck*, I bet she looks so good from your angle, huh?"

Harrow doesn't reply, making me wonder if it's a rhetorical question. But a few seconds later he moves his foot back, giving me hope that I can sit the hell up and stop with this humiliation.

Until he shifts his other boot, placing it expectantly just under my face on the dirty cement. I don't even look up at him. I can feel the embarrassment burning my face, and I know I'm probably red as hell as I give the same treatment to this boot.

Finally he reaches down again, dragging me up to my knees even though I can't meet his eyes. "Don't you have something to say to me?" Harrow asks patiently, his grip in my hair is firm and unyielding. When I look up at him, a baleful expression in my eyes, he chuckles. "I'll help you out before you say something I'll make you regret. This is where you thank me, little girl."

"For what?" I snap before I can stop myself.

"For letting you lick my boots. Unless you want to do it again until you find a reason to be grateful."

I definitely don't want to do that. Not with the continued taste of leather lingering on my tongue and embarrassment burning in my face. But thanking him is almost just as humiliating. "Thank you," I whisper finally, not looking at him.

"Do better." Harrow shakes me by the hair like a dog. "I know you can do better."

"*Thank you*," I hiss, glaring up at him. But the warning in his eyes makes me drop my shoulders, and I widen my eyes instead. "Thank you," I murmur, reaching out to press a hand gently to his thigh. "For letting me appreciate your boots. I—You were right. I really like them, and they were super distracting earlier in the lobby."

"Good girl. See?" He lets go of me, lifting one foot to shove me back onto my thighs. "I knew you could do it."

Before I can even move, Ravage is there, dragging me up by my hoodie and across the floor amidst my shrieks of protest. He tosses me onto the mattress, following me down onto it a second later to cage me in.

"Oh, you can fight me all you want, princess," he laughs, grabbing my wrists and slamming them to the mattress over my head as I go to grab him. "I like it. It's so *fun* when you're fiery." He grips the hem of my hoodie in one hand, shoving it up my body.

"Stop!" I protest, lashing out at him and managing to knee him in the hip. "I don't—" But he's definitely not giving me a choice. In seconds, he wrestles my hoodie off of me, his grip shifting to pin me to the bed by my throat.

"God, you're so fucking gorgeous." His other hand is bare and strokes down my chest, brushing over the swell of my breasts before pressing down against my hips. "So gorgeous that I don't think I want to share you. Well..." He glances over his shoulder as Harrow drops to sit at the side of the mattress, watching carefully. "I'll share you with him, but that's only because we share everything. Anyone else, though?" He shakes his head. "I don't think that would be okay, princess. You get it."

"I really don't." I kick out at him again and both of them move. Harrow grabs my wrists and pins them as he slides behind me to pull me back against his chest. "What are you doing?" I sneer at him, though when he *looks* at me I shy away, dropping my gaze to his hands.

"At least you know who to be afraid of," he chuckles, wrapping an arm around me to pin my arms at my sides.

Ravage kneels between my knees, not letting me press my thighs together. He reaches up to stroke his fingers down my thighs, moving to grab the heel of my sneaker in one hand and yanking it off. I fight him for the other, but soon enough it's on the floor with the first, with Ravage's fingers tangled in the fabric of my leggings.

"You're going to fight me for them, huh?" he laughs. "You're going to be such a bitch about me pulling them down, I just know it. But that's okay." He doesn't try to pull them down. He reaches up to grip the waistband, *yanking* on it until I hear the fabric ripping down the seam.

And he makes it look so easy. Even though I'm writhing and fighting against Harrow's hold, Ravage just rips my leggings apart like it's one of the easiest things he's done all day. As I watch, they're reduced to stripes of fabric, and he easily yanks them off of my ankles to toss the ruined clothing somewhere else.

Leaving me only in my Ghostface mask underwear.

"Oh, now that is just adorable. How *precious*," Ravage purrs. He trails his fingers up my thighs, hooking his fingers in my underwear and dragging them down as well. "Do we have a little horror lover? Are we making this *real* enough for you?"

"Fuck you," I hiss, though there's a lot less bite in my words than before as I try to press my thighs together to hide myself from him.

"Yeah." Ravage laughs, his fingers digging into my thighs. "That's absolutely the plan, princess." He plunges two fingers into me without warning, groaning at the feeling of my pussy clenching down around him. "You're still loose for me," he purrs in approval. "I knew it was worth it to finger your pretty pussy earlier. God." He scissors his fingers and pulls away, reaching up only to smear his fingers across my cheek. "She doesn't even need me to prep her, Harrow. She's begging for it."

"Maybe for you." Without warning, Harrow shoves me forward, forcing me onto my knees until Ravage can grab my hair to keep me on all fours. He moves behind me, and I hear the buckle of his belt clink as he undoes it and slides down his zipper again.

Remembering how intimidating he'd felt in my mouth, I whimper, glancing up at Ravage as if he has any intention of helping me out. "Don't," I murmur, trying to tug free. "Please, I—"

"It's a bit late for that." Ravage's voice is rough with excitement, and he undoes his own belt with hurried motions, able to do it with one hand as he settles back on his heels, thighs spread, to unzip his cargo pants as well. "Come here, gorgeous girl." He's barely freed his half-hard length as he drags my face down to him, not giving me a moment before he's sliding his tip against my lower lip.

"Don't be shy now. I might not be wearing the pretty boots like Harrow, but you can show me how much you love my cock anyway, can't you?" His grip in my hair is tight, as his fingers scrape against my scalp.

I really don't know what else to do, unless I want to bite him. But that definitely feels like it'll get me murdered. Not to mention...I swallow hard, fighting the rise of anticipation in my body and the tinge of heat between my thighs.

I *definitely* shouldn't be into this. At all.

Opening my mouth, I lick at his tip, realizing he's giving me the time to do what I want instead of shoving himself between my lips like Harrow had done. He shudders under my tongue, and boldly I lick a stripe up the underside of his cock to the sound of his moans.

But I've forgotten Harrow, somehow. At least until his hands find my hips, making me flinch, and he runs his hands down my thighs, then smooths them up over my ass.

"Relax." I hear him murmur. "I'm not trying to hurt you, Noa." He moves closer to my entrance every time his gloves stroke against me, teasing me and threatening me at the same time.

"Put it in your mouth, princess," Ravage growls hoarsely. "I'm tired of you teasing me." I do what he says, sinking down with his length against my tongue until he bumps the back of my throat.

Harrow takes that moment to slide two fingers into me, drawing a sound from my throat that must be good for Ravage, given how he curses under his breath.

"You were right, I suppose." Harrow's voice is so...uncaring. Just so *bland* as he remarks on my body. "Usually you rush things. I figured you were lying to me about her being ready to take us. But"—he adds another finger, ignoring my whine of protest—"you were right this time."

"I'm always right—Fuck, princess. Your mouth feels so

good." He thrusts up against my lips. "Can you take more for me, sweetheart?"

"She can take all of you." Harrow's fingers are suddenly gone, and I can't help the whimper of frustration that sounds too loudly in the space between us. Kindly, they don't remark on it. I can feel Harrow shifting on the bed behind me, his hands coming up to stroke my hips again. "Just relax for me. Like I said, little girl, I'm not trying to hurt you." I feel the brush of him against me, and it's torture that I can't see him as he slides his cock between my folds.

"Is she wet for you?"

"Oh, she's very into this." Harrow teases me with his tip, barely entering me before he once again just slides his cock between my parted thighs. "Relax," he murmurs again, stroking his fingers down my spine. "Don't want you tensing up or biting Ravage. I don't think he'll like that." His hand splays against my lower back, holding me in place, and he presses into me, his cock stretching my walls and sinking deep into my body without stopping.

He's so big that it gets uncomfortable quickly. But even when I whine in protest, he doesn't stop. The only time he does go still is when he's buried as deep as he can go inside of me, his hips pressed flush against the backs of my thighs.

Ravage's hand flexes in my hair. "Does her pussy feel as good as I'm dreaming it does?" he asks, moving my head however he wants. It's just as embarrassing as everything else, to have him fucking himself with my mouth and just *using* me like this.

It really shouldn't be so hot. I definitely shouldn't be into this at all, and it's hard to focus on the burn of discomfort when the feeling of being full is so *satisfying*.

Sex has never been like this for me before. But then again,

I've never been fucked by two murderers on a filthy mattress in a warehouse before. Maybe this is just my kink.

A very *problematic* kink.

"Better." Harrow pulls back to thrust into me hard, dragging a yelp from my throat. "She's so greedy for me. Whenever I pull out..." He does it again as if illustrating his point, before slamming back into me. "She clenches down around me. *Greedy.*" But he says it like praise, holding me in place with his hand on my back while he fucks me.

It's hard to focus on just that, however. Especially when Ravage gets more insistent, dragging me up and down by my hair and making me choke on his cock. "Good girl," he praises, his voice breathy. "Mmm, that's such a good girl. You're just such a perfect play toy for us, aren't you, princess?"

I can't answer, but I doubt that he really wants me to. The two of them talk over me, my brain fogging up a little bit at the dual stimulation of being fucked and having Ravage fucking my mouth. It's a new feeling to feel this floaty during sex, or at all, and I can't help it when I relax into both of them, something inside of me seeming to unwind as I start to enjoy it.

"There you go." Harrow's words are a growl of approval. "Look at you being so good for us."

"*Fuck*, I want to come in her pussy," Ravage whines. "This is so unfair."

Harrow's soft laugh meets my ears, but I'm barely listening to their words. They banter back and forth, until suddenly I'm jerked upward to my knees, my lips parted as I register the absence of Ravage's cock.

Harrow sits up as well, his cock slipping free from me, and turns me to face him. "Oh..." His eyes narrow behind his mask. "Well, well. Look at you, Noa."

Ravage rests his head on my shoulder, tilting his chin questioningly.

"Our little girl is in subspace, aren't you?" Harrow croons, but he's obviously not expecting an answer. He drags me down over him, laying down on the bed with his hands on my hips. "Come on. You can have it back. Take my cock like a good girl." He urges me down, one hand going down to position himself so that when he presses me against him, his cock slides back inside of me, pulling a groan from my lips.

"Just like that." He starts fucking me again, hands on my hips as he rolls his hips up, grinding into me.

"*Fuck*," Ravage growls. "Don't let her look back at me, okay?" His words only make me want to look more, but Harrow reaches up, grabbing my face in both hands to make me look down at his mask with the red-painted upside down cross on his forehead.

The first touch of Ravage's tongue on my inner thigh makes me flinch in surprise, and I buck my hips, trying and failing to turn to look at him while Harrow laughs. He does it again, his tongue lapping at my entrance that's stretched around Harrow's cock. Judging by the shudder that goes through the man under me, I have a feeling Ravage's tongue isn't only on me.

"Rav..." Harrow's voice is low, and there's definitely a warning in it. The man behind me chuckles, his hands coming up to stroke over my hips.

"I'm gonna need you to be so good for us, princess," Ravage murmurs, the feel of the latex of his mask on my shoulder proving that he's put it back on. "I promise it'll be so good for you. Even though it'll definitely hurt at first."

I blink a few times, trying to form a coherent thought while Harrow thrusts slowly, languidly into me. "What..." But I don't need to finish the question when I feel Ravage's fingers stroke along my folds, finger dipping into me beside Harrow's cock.

"N-no!" I protest, trying to jerk away only for Harrow to drag me back down.

"Don't be like that," Ravage croons. He adds another finger, sliding them alongside Harrow's cock. "You don't have to be so scared, princess. I know what I'm doing, and I promise you can handle this if you just relax for me." He continues to force me to take his fingers, moving them with Harrow's thrusts before finally pulling them free.

"I can't," I gasp, fighting against Harrow's grip on my hair and hip. "That's—I *really can't*—"

"You really can," Ravage growls. "I wouldn't lie to you. Just...relax." He grabs my thighs, holding me in place. At the first brush of his cock along my folds, I sob, sinking into Harrow's hold until my face is buried in his throat.

A shudder goes through me, but I try my hardest not to tense up. Pleading whines leave my mouth, though I hear Harrow's soft words of consolation and encouragement as Ravage slowly works his cock into me beside Harrow's; my head spins at the feeling of being stretched by both of them.

I can feel it when he's fully sheathed inside of me, and I can *hear* his groan of pleasure, his fingers digging into my hips. "Oh *fuck*, you're perfect. How can you be this perfect, Noa?" He says a few other things, but my heartbeat in my ears is overwhelming, making it so I can barely hear their words through the noise.

"It's too much," I whine into Harrow's throat, face still pressed to his neck. "It's *way* too much, please!"

"Oh, but baby...the hard part's over. Why are you protesting now?" He thrusts experimentally, dragging a harsh cry from my lips as I shudder. "If it was really too much, you would've been protesting a lot more before. But *now*?" He pushes into me again, and Harrow's movements pick up once more, until they're both fucking my cunt.

"Well, now we can both see how much you like this. How much you clearly need two cocks in your greedy little pussy." His laugh is rough and dark against my shoulder, his grip bruising as he picks up his pace. My head spins at the feeling of both of them fucking me, both of them in my pussy and sliding against each other.

It seems impossible. It seems like it should be *painful*.

What's way worse is how much I like it. How quickly the pain is fading to pleasure as heat curls and twists up my spine. Before I know it, I'm not whimpering for them to stop.

I'm whimpering for them to keep going.

Ravage is easily the less controlled of them. His thrusts are eager, erratic, and I can feel his impatience as he chases his release.

"I bet you'll look so good with your pussy full of our cum," he growls against my spine. "I bet we could keep you like this —full and needy and *begging* for more. You know…" His fingers trail down my spine until he's teasing just over my tailbone. "I bet I could ruin this pretty ass of yours, too. Bet I could make you *beg* for me to ruin all of your greedy holes."

His words are only making my stomach and pussy clench tighter. Harrow doesn't seem to mind how I'm panting and probably crying into his neck at the overstimulation of them both fucking me. He's content to thrust into me with the occasional praising murmur against my throat.

I like it when they talk about me. I like it even more when they talk *to each other* about me, like it's not worth considering my opinion.

Ravage's thrusts start stuttering first. He definitely has the lesser self control of either of them, and soon enough he's dropping praises from his lips and clenching my hips tightly in his grip as his cock slides alongside Harrow's.

"*Fuck*," he snarls against my shoulder blade. "You feel so

fucking good...It's crazy how your pussy is made for us, you know that?" There's a breathy note in his voice, and I can tell as he gets closer by his breathing. He snarls against my skin, slamming into me one more time and shuddering as he comes.

Not that Harrow seems to be in any hurry. He reaches up to brush his fingers down Ravage's arm, watching him with narrowed eyes while Ravage snarls and growls like a wild, feral thing.

He's not paying attention to me, I realize, barely able to see him draped over my back from where I'm between them. But I can tell he's half out of it, and I can't help the way my fingers inch up toward his head that's resting at my shoulder.

It would be just so easy to tug off his mask. My fingers brush the plastic as he growls, not noticing what I'm doing, and I'm convinced Harrow is too busy fucking me and touching Ravage to notice either.

But the moment my fingers clamp down on the material, ready to tug, Harrow strikes, quick as a snake, to grip my waist.

"Oh, no you don't, little girl," he growls in my ear, forcing me to sit up in his lap as Ravage falls back on his heels. "That was *really* bad of you. I thought we were making progress on the good choices, but..."

His grip tightens on my arm, eyes pinning mine. "I guess you'll have to learn the hard way."

10

"I'm sorry," I whine, staring up at Harrow's mask. "I just wanted to fucking *see* him, okay? And you, obviously, by extension. You really think I'd go to the cops?" I fix him with a look that's part pleading and part skepticism, but it doesn't sway him. I can see it in his eyes.

"You're really *not* sorry." But I can hear the humor in his voice. "And I don't trust you, Noa. Who knows what you'd do or say just to get away from us. But if someone has to teach you how to make good decisions, then I don't mind being that person." Ravage reaches up from behind me, wrapping his fingers around my throat, only for Harrow to make a noise of disapproval.

"Stop." His voice is flat, eyes on mine. "She likes that too much. I can see it on her face. Go *sit*, you're done anyway." There's no room for argument in his tone, but I hear Ravage's grumble behind me as he slides free of me, gets up off the bed and strides over to collapse in the old, threadbare armchair.

Harrow watches him, only looking back at me when he's satisfied. "This doesn't have to be that bad," he informs me, reaching up to press his fingers sweetly to my jaw. I lean into him nervously, letting him cradle my face in his hand.

"Please don't stab me. Or, okay..." I can feel the nervous rambling coming back, panic bubbling in my chest. "I'd rather you stab me than do anything involving a chainsaw. Also, Clown Mask Girl skewered some eyes and handed one to me. I didn't realize it was real at the time but—" I suck in a breath, trying not to go down that tangent. "All I'm asking is no chainsaws and nothing with my eyes. I'm actually pretty attached to them."

With a snort, Harrow rolls his eyes. "Don't worry, I'm also pretty attached to your eyes," he points out. "I like how you look at me when you're begging for something. I'm not going to kill you, little girl. What would be the lesson in that? I'm going to teach you about consequences." His grip tightening on my face is the only warning I get before I'm suddenly face down over his lap, his cock brushing against my skin and my face in the worn blanket under him.

My head spins, and I try to figure out what's going on as Harrow situates me more comfortably over his thighs, dragging his fingers down my spine. When I try to sit up, he just clicks his tongue at me and shoves me right back down.

"If I have to let Rav come back over here to hold you down, it'll be worse," he informs me, his tone full of warning. "So, are you going to stay for me like a good girl?"

I don't know what's going on, or how it could be worse, but I don't think I want to find out. I nod fervently against the blanket, sucking in a breath through my nose as I brace one knee under me for leverage.

As if I'm going anywhere.

"I know you just want to see. You're so curious, aren't you? That's what got you into this whole mess, in the first place." He sounds so pitying. So *condescending*, and it makes me squirm, the feeling strange and not all bad. "Yeah, I see you. I know you like being talked to this way. We'll have to explore that another time, won't we? This is a *punishment*, Noa." There's a reprimand in his voice, but with the blood rushing in my ears, I can barely bring myself to care.

His fingers stroke up my thighs, and finally he lays his palm flat against my ass, making me tense. Suddenly, I have a pretty good idea of what his punishment is, and I'm not sure I like it. I take a few breaths, trying not to let my heart race its way to an early failure, while Harrow just murmurs soothingly to me and rests his hand where it is.

"You're going to count for me. How many do you think she deserves, Rav? It was your mask, after all?"

I can't look up to see Ravage somewhere behind me, but I hear him shift on his little throne. "Five," he says finally. "She just wanted to *see*."

Harrow huffs out a laugh. "You're way too soft. *And* too attached. We'll have to talk about that later. Ten," he declares after a moment of thought. "I don't think that's too much to give her."

"Ten? For wanting to see my *face*? Come on, Harrow." It's an interesting feeling to have Ravage on my side. And an unexpected occurrence I hadn't expected.

"*You're* about to get twenty if you don't shut up." Harrow's retort is sharp, and from Ravage's silence, I figure he's not bluffing. He flexes his fingers against my skin, dragging his nails over the curve of my ass, before his hand disappears and I tense.

"No, don't do that. You're fine. I promise, you'll be more than fine. Will you count for me, pretty girl? Out loud?" It's not a question, not really. But I nod anyway in answer, turning my head to the side to gaze across the room where I can see Ravage's shorter boots.

Harrow doesn't hesitate. His palm comes down hard and hot against my skin, pulling a yelp from my throat and causing me to buck up against him in instinctive protest. But he pushes me back down with his hand on the back of my neck, his touch gentle and patient. When I don't say anything, it's Rav who coughs pointedly.

"One," I say quickly, remembering finally what I'm supposed to be doing.

"Good girl." I love Harrow's soft murmur, and when his hand makes contact with my skin again, I only whine and shudder, instead of trying to fly away.

"Two," I whisper, counting out the next two as well as my head begins to spin.

After number five, his hand comes back down softly, fingers stroking the overheated, tender skin and making me squirm against his thighs. "Not so bad, is it?" he purrs. "You're doing so well for me, Noa. But I knew you would. You take everything we give you so well. Five more, darling. Then you're done and I'll make you come on my cock."

His next few hits are on the backs of my thighs, which hurts in a different way and have me sobbing in protest while forcing myself to count those out as well. Finally, I gasp out the word *ten*, chest heaving and head spinning wildly. The pain is hot and sharp, and when I realize I'm grinding down against his thigh, I'm mortified with myself.

"You can thank me now." His voice is flat and expectant, leaving no room for argument. He's not joking. But then, he never seems to joke.

"Thank you," I murmur without complaint, flinching under his soft touches on my thighs.

"Oh, that was so easy. You learn so well. You can just lie there for me. Just breathe, okay? You did so well for me." His fingers brush between my thighs, teasingly at first, before he slips two digits into me. "And so wet for me still? I think you might be into this, Noa. Hmm?" He twists his fingers, thrusting them in and out of my sore pussy easily, like he has all the time in the world. "Yeah, precious girl. I really think you're into this. Come on. Sit up."

He gently pulls me upright, his sudden sweetness is just as confusing as everything else. He pulls me over his lap, forcing me to straddle his thighs, and reaches out to gently wipe away the tears rolling down my cheeks. "You can cry for me," he promises. "I won't tell you not to. Cry for me all you want, okay?" His grip doesn't give me a choice of where to go or how to move. He urges me down on my back, pinning me there with his hands braced on either side of my head. "Good girl." God, I love it when he praises me. Just those words have a shiver going down my spine, and he reaches out once more, tugging my thigh up over his hip.

When he thrusts into me, it's a smooth, controlled motion, and he doesn't pause until he's buried in me. I can't help the sound that escapes my lips at the feeling of him fucking my sore pussy again. "Look at Ravage," he orders, his voice low and rough. "I want him to see your face and see how fast I can have you begging for me."

Braced on one arm, he holds onto my hip as he fucks me, his thrusts measured and harsh as he drives into me over and over, making me see stars almost every time. His hand leaves my hip after a minute or so, sliding between us so he can rub my clit with his thumb.

"Don't!" I gasp suddenly, arching off the bed while staring wide-eyed at Ravage. It takes me a moment to register that his cargo pants are still undone, and he's gently sliding his fingers up and down his cock.

"Why?" Harrow asks, not stopping. "You love it."

"It's too much." I'm so on edge, so fucking ready to come, it feels like every single movement is about to throw me over the edge. As if his spanking me didn't deter how much I'm into this, but pushed me further toward my release.

But that's a self-introspective problem for another time. For now, I squirm against him, my hands coming up to grip the fabric of his shirt, bunching the material up against his shoulders. "There you go," he urges, slamming into me with a growl. "You can hold on to me, Noa. Dig your nails in if you need to. You're so perfect for me. And look how much he wants you."

I open my eyes again, gaze fixed on Ravage as he starts to jerk himself off in earnest, even though I'm sure he's still oversensitive from coming not too long ago. But if that's a problem for him, he doesn't seem to mind.

Whimpers pour from my lips, louder and louder as Harrow fucks me. "I'm—" I take a breath and look up at him, twisting his shirt between my fingers. "Harrow, I'm—"

"So come for me, my desperate, gorgeous girl," he snarls in a rough voice. "Come on my cock like my good little girl. My *perfect* little plaything. Come on. I won't ask again..." His thumb moves faster, putting more pressure on my clit, and I can't help feeling like his goading has a lot to do with the fact that I'm arching off the mattress into him, eyes closing hard as my orgasm rips through me.

Harrow fucks me through it, fucks me while my head spins and I drag in deep, panting breaths. He doesn't stop, instead opting to hold me down with his other hand at the base of my throat so I can't move away from him.

It quickly becomes too much. I sob out a plea, begging him to stop. But he's deaf to my words until he's forced me into another orgasm that's on the edge of being painful.

"Please!" I sob, eyes open to meet his gaze. "Harrow, please! I can't—"

"Oh, I think you most certainly can if I tell you to. I want to feel that pussy clench around my cock one more time. You hear me, Noa?" His grip shifts, fingers tightening around my throat just like Rav's had earlier. "You're going to come for me *one more time*." His harsh, almost cruel thrusts and his fingers on my clit don't leave me much of a choice. This time it *does* hurt, and I scream around my desperate release that's torn from me, no matter how much I try to fight it.

My body aches, protesting, as Harrow slams into me one last time, snarling out a few curses and praises in quick succession as he trembles between my thighs.

"Good girl. Such a good girl for me." He's panting, his grip on my throat is trembling, as he throws his head back to ride out the rest of his orgasm. It takes me longer for my head to stop spinning, and I let out a too-needy whine when he slips free of me, dropping my leg to the bed so I can relax against the old blanket.

"I'm happy you fucked up," Harrow admits, sitting back on his heels before getting to his feet. I roll over to my side to watch him as he strides past Ravage in his chair, hand coming out to stroke along his chest affectionately before he heads for a table in the corner. "Neither of us would've had this kind of fun if you'd gone to *Grim Descent* like you should've."

I don't reply, I can't find the words to. I feel too spacey, too foggy, to do more than watch him as I try to drag my soul back down to my body where it belongs.

God, I'm already so sore.

When Harrow turns around, a cloth in his hand, a jolt of panic goes through me. I sit up, scooting back to the wall to press my back against it. As if having my back to a wall is going to help me whatsoever. "What are you doing?" I ask, toes curling against the mattress.

Ravage gets up as well, striding over to drop beside me. Before I can bolt, he wraps his arms around my shoulders, dragging me against his chest. "You're okay," he murmurs from behind his mask. "Don't freak out, Noa. Everything is just how it's supposed to be. You should've known we couldn't let you walk out of here tonight."

"N-no. But…" I look between them, pressing myself harder to the wall as Harrow comes back to sit on the mattress. "Please don't," I whisper, trying to pull away from Ravage. I yank on his arms, nails digging into his skin and causing him to hiss in discomfort.

"Consequences of our actions, precious girl," Harrow reminds me, eyes dark behind his mask. "You came here tonight, where you were not invited. You didn't leave when we gave you every chance and every reason to. Instead, you stayed. This is on you, not us."

"I didn't do anything wrong," I whisper, shoving away from him and into Ravage's chest. But Ravage only wraps his arms around me tightly, shushing me softly as he rocks me back and forth on the bed.

This time, the tears on my cheeks aren't from pleasure or overstimulation. This time, I'm crying because Harrow is going to kill me. "Please don't," I beg again, wishing I knew the magic words to get me out of this. "I'll—"

"Your begging is wasted on me this time, gorgeous girl," Harrow says, an apology in his words. "This is how tonight was always going to end." He reaches out to tuck my hair behind my ear, and I sob in earnest, shrinking away from him as fear pounds through my veins in freezing waves.

I don't want to die.

I don't want to fucking die.

With Ravage shifting to pin my arms against my sides, there's no way for me to fight either of them. And even though I try to hold my breath when Harrow presses the cloth over my mouth and nose, he's much more patient than me.

Certainly patient enough to wait me out until my brain forces me to take a deep inhale that has my head spinning instantly. Then my eyes go up to his in a silent, desperate plea for mercy.

But he doesn't comply. He's not moved by it, and he only tilts his head to the side as my world goes dark. The animal skull mask is the last thing I get to see before consciousness leaves me fully and I'm slumped into Ravage's hold as the world goes dark and empty.

11

My first thought is that if this is the afterlife, there really shouldn't be cell phones. Certainly not ones that vibrate and screech like mine is doing from the nightstand.

My second thought is filled with shock at the fact I'm waking up *at all*. When I was getting knocked out, I'd been sure that would be it. That if I woke up, it would be chained to a chair with a chainsaw in my face.

Not in my own bed.

Sitting up quickly proves to be a mistake, and I groan as every single inch of my body protests. "Fuck..." I groan, falling back down on my bed and flexing my fingers while my phone continues to yell at me. "I know. I hear you," I mumble, and blink up at my lazily spinning ceiling fan. In theory, I have to be alive. I ache too much to be dead, I hope.

Finally, I reach out for my phone, fingers curling around it as I drag it back to me. It's with a heavy, frustrated sigh, however, that I flop over onto my side and look at the screen to see who's been calling me.

It's Sierra, naturally. Seventy-two calls, forty-seven texts, and twelve voicemails stare at me from the screen, and I definitely have no intention of listening to the voice messages. I don't need to. Even without the texts, I would have a pretty good idea of what she wants.

Clearly, she thinks I'm dead. A groan escapes my lips as I unlock my phone, registering a bit late that it's plugged in and charged.

But I certainly hadn't done it. I'd been *out*.

I'm alive. I send the message to the group chat, and immediately Sienna is typing back, screaming random letters at me and trying to call again. But I decline it this time, mouth twitching in a frown.

I'll call you in a bit. Gotta get up first. I know she has questions. I get that. But I hit send and toss my phone on the bed before forcing myself to sit up despite the aches and pains. "God, I feel eighty," I sigh, pressing my palms to my face. Belatedly, I realize that I'm only in my hoodie. No bra, no leggings—if there's anything left of them—and no underwear. No shoes, either, but when I glance down at the floor beside my bed, I see them resting neatly on my floor.

Bloody and stained.

They're not going to be salvageable.

"So much for my new shoes." I push to my feet with a huff and walk across the room while my body screams at me to lay the fuck down and go back to sleep. I'm so tired, even though I've just woken up, and I almost dread flipping on the bathroom light so I can see myself in the mirror.

But I do it anyway. I have no choice, really.

My breath catches in my throat at the sight of my pale, tired face. My hair is a mess, and the dark circles under my eyes are so bad that I might as well invest in a concealer company for a lifetime supply. I reach up, fingers brushing over my throat and the fingerprint-shaped bruises that bloom starkly against my skin. "Fuck," I murmur, but I can't deny the thrilling shiver that travels up my spine.

"*Fuck*." I almost laugh incredulously as I lift up my hoodie to look at my chest and stomach. More bruises litter my hips and sides, in the shape of varying fingerprints. Last, I tug off my hoodie entirely, pushing my hair back over my shoulder to look at my neck and shoulders clearly.

I look...*awful*.

Along with the fingerprints, there are multiple bite marks and hickeys staining my skin. My fingers brush over them, tracing the still-tender marks almost reverently. But I'm not upset by them. How can I be? They go along sweetly with the ache between my thighs that tells me I'd *really* gone beyond my comfort zone last night.

Not that Harrow and Ravage had really given me a *choice*.

Not that I mind right now, truth be told.

I stare at myself for another few seconds, wondering how many more marks I'll find on my body as the day goes on. After all, there's a lot of me I can't see in the mirror, and sometimes bruises take a little longer to form on me.

While there's something like delight in my chest as I bite my lower lip thoughtfully, I know for a *fact* I won't be leaving my apartment for the next few days. There's no way I could even go to Starbucks without someone calling the cops on me for some kind of home checkup.

I look like a victim of a crime.

And, okay, I kind of am.

The thought brings a laugh to my lips, and my mouth curves in a nervous, secret smile while I lean on my hands with my face pressed close to the mirror. "You're really fucked up," I murmur to my reflection. "And the worst part..." I tilt my head, studying my face and my light blue eyes in the mirror. "You miss them already."

Sure, I'm grateful. Really grateful to be alive. But I know I'll never find anyone like them in my real life, in the daytime. They only exist behind Halloween masks and in the dark, where I'd found them. But the disappointment is bitter as hell as I push off of my counter and walk back into my room.

My phone rings again as I'm throwing on a loose, long-sleeved tee and shorts that just barely cover the bruises on my thighs. I can't help rolling my eyes, a little irritated Sierra couldn't wait five fucking minutes for me to call her back.

Sure enough, when I cross the room and snatch my phone up from my pillow to unplug it from the charger, the name on the screen is hers. I accept the call, putting the phone to my ear and greeting her with, "I told you I'd call you—"

"*What the hell happened to you?!*" I've never heard her scream at me, and I jerk the phone away from my ear, nose curled in distaste. "*Where the fuck were you? Do you know how worried we've been? We called the cops, but they said you weren't missing yet. We-we looked everywhere for you, Noa!*"

"Sorry," I murmur, feeling a little guilty. From my nightstand I swipe a bottle of ibuprofen, shaking out four and swallowing them dry like a pro. It's a mistake, though, I realize as my sore throat protests and it takes a few extra swallows to make sure everything makes it down without getting stuck or ejecting from my esophagus. "Just...stuff happened, and I lost my phone. You were right, I was in the wrong place. I, umm..." She's going to want a better explanation than that. And maybe I owe her one, seeing as I'd ruined her night.

But God, I'm so worn out. All I want to do is curl up on my couch with my cats under a comforter, and maybe order an emotional support pie to be delivered here.

"*What happened?*" Sierra demands again. "*How the hell did you lose your phone?*"

I decide instantly to give her the truth. Or as much of it as I can...which isn't much at all. "I was at a different haunt. They took my phone, since they were only doing one more run. I thought you guys were just lost or at the wrong place, and I didn't want to miss out. I, uh." I curl my toes against the floor, staring down at the light grey carpet. "Then I met a couple of guys. And uh, sort of lost track of time." It's basically the truth, since I hadn't had my phone on me, or possessed any other way to tell the time.

"*...You're joking.*" Sierra's words are flat and she's quiet as I make my way out of my room and through the living room where two of my cats are lounging on the sofa. The third, a fluffy black menace, is curled up on my counter, staring at me with narrow yellow eyes. He knows he shouldn't be up there. But here we are, doing it anyway. But it's pretty typical of Finn.

"I am not joking." Standing on my tiptoes, I grab a mug out of the cabinet of my favorites, setting it on the stove as I debate the merits of making coffee versus just ordering it along with groceries. I could *really* go for a peppermint white mocha to go along with the pecan pie I intend to order for myself to eat today.

A knock on my door makes me glance toward the stairs that lead to the first floor, where my door and the door to the apartment below me are. "That's not you at my door, right?" I ask, wondering if it's someone mistaking me for my downstairs neighbor *again*.

"*No, but, umm...*" The guilty tone of her voice immediately puts me on edge. "*The cops said they'd do a wellness check on you at your apartment this morning. I gave them your address...In my defense, I really thought you were dead or in some sort of fugue state, okay?*" She's getting more and more defensive the longer she talks, but I'm too frustrated to care.

"Of course you have them doing a wellness check," I mutter. "Because this morning needed to be more stressful." She apologizes as I walk down the stairs, quicker than normal in my need to get rid of the police at my door. "I swear, I'm putting you on speaker," I threaten, noticing that my door isn't locked. That's...dangerous. But also maybe not that unexpected, given that there's only one way I'd gotten back here in the early hours of this morning. "I'm putting you on speaker so that you can tell them—" I yank the door open, eyes falling on the two men who stand at my door.

Except...they aren't cops.

The two men look effortlessly comfortable on my small front porch, and the shorter one leans against the doorframe, sweeping a hand through his auburn hair as a grin dances on his face. I notice his palm is bandaged, and his wrist looks worse for wear. He smiles at me, bright green eyes glittering as I stare at him. "Hi there," he purrs in a voice that's incredibly familiar. "You look better than I expected."

"I..." I just stand there, in basically my pajamas, with my hair a complete mess, and stare at the faces of the two men who fucked me within an inch of my life last night.

"*Noa?*" Worry seeps into Sierra's voice. "*What's wrong? Is it the police—*"

"I'll take care of it. Don't worry, Sierra. I just—I'll take care of it." I hang up on her amidst her protests, hand falling to my side as I clutch my phone, unsure of what to do.

"Are you going to let us in, sweetheart?" the other man asks, his voice just as soft and velvety as it had been when he'd been wearing the animal skull mask. His dark eyes rest on mine, never once moving as I look him over, from his well fitting jeans to his sharp cheekbones and curling, black hair.

He's taller than his partner, and definitely the more terrifying of the two, even in the daylight. "Because you can stare at us inside just as well as out here."

"And I'm hungry," the auburn-haired man complains. "So what'll it be, Noa?" He leans in and gently, so fucking gently, tilts my head up to his even as the black-haired man reaches out to tug my phone out of my grip.

"Will you let us in to play?"

ABOUT THE AUTHOR

AJ Merlin would rather write epic love stories than live them. I mean, who wants to limit themselves to only falling in love once? She is obsessed with dark fantasy, true crime, and also dogs. From serial killers to voyeurs all the way down to the devil himself, AJ's specialty is in writing irredeemable heroes who somehow still manage to captivate their heroines (and her readers).